BRICK

Fire Lake – Book 1

M. Tasia

ALSO BY M. TASIA

The Boys of Brighton series
Gabe
Sam's Soldiers
Rick's Bear
Jesse
Coop
Travis
Grady
Vincent
Shadow
The Holidays

The Gates series
Saint
Finn
James
Joey
Bradley
Carlos
Sawyer
Trey

EVERYONE LOVES THE BOYS OF BRIGHTON

"I loved this book and I love this town. I hope there's going to be more."
—Melissa Lemons on *Gabe*

"An amazing read that was filled with lust, love, crazy hot sex, danger, action and so much more This is the first book I have read in this series but I will definitely be reading more in the future."
—Gay Book Reviews on *Sam's Soldiers*

"I was crazy impressed that the author made me teary over the ending of a relationship that I shouldn't have even been invested in. I didn't yet know these characters yet the author made me hurt for them. That takes some mad writing skills!"
—Love Bytes Reviews

"Jesse and Royce together have my heart. Jesse has it all by himself."
—The Book Junkie Reads on *Jesse*

"So much action, intrigue, drama and angst for the long awaited story of Grady and Ben. This was worth the wait. Sexy and sweet. I can't wait for the next."
—SamD on *Grady*

"I knew this one would be my favorite to date! There was something about Vincent that said awesome then came Tristan."
—Booky on *Vincent*

"This installment of the Boys of Brighton was so good! I loved Shadow and Randy 's story I was hooked from the first page to the last. This book was definitely worth the wait!"
—AG on *Shadow*

"I have loved this series from the very first story and this holiday novella is simply perfect. We get a glimpse of all our couples and

what is happening in their lives while the holidays explode around them. I cannot wait for more!"
—bookobsessed on *The Holidays*

ANOTHER BIG LOVE – THE GATES

"Ms. Tasia has done it again! This is Saint's story, for readers of the Brighton Boys, you'll know he needs a break! After being forced to become a plastic surgeon by his father, he rebels by assisting people in 3rd world countries, which puts him in the position to be kidnapped and tortured. You really feel for him, that's for sure! Max is the perfect man for poor Saint's battered soul, not that he doesn't have his own issues! Overall, this was engaging, steady paced and chock full of all the feels!"
—Avid Reader on *Saint*

"Finn and Miguel stole my heart. This is a great Sunday afternoon read. Finn's character jumped off the page as his story developed through each chapter. I loved reading his truth and watching him and Miguel find their home in each other."
—K.A. Brown on *Finn*

"This is really a great series and I def recommend it. I loved James and Ross, it was a rough start for the two, but they worked it out. I can't wait for more, love everything M. TASIA writes!"
—TammyKay on *James*

"I may have my new favorite book couple of the series. Joey and Sam just have that something special. At one point I was ugly crying but it was a good ugly cry if that makes any sense. I really love the series and I can't wait for her next installment!!"
—Vine Voice on *Joey*

"This author is really talented and I love her series, this one and the Boys of Brighton. Her characters are so well drawn and I can really get into the stories. I especially loved Eric in this particular book.

I'm hoping Clay the rookie will be the next book. Keep 'em coming!"
—Rosemary on *Bradley*

"Two men with damaged souls come together and find love. A tried and true formula that works well here, especially when working with two lovable characters like Carlos and Clay. Carlos especially was interesting to me - the contrast of his appearance to his gentle nature, a true gentle giant. And Clay being all protective of the much larger, but more gentle man - so sweet! I really liked this story and am looking forward to more of The Gates now."
—Valeen on *Carlos*

"Sawyer is the newest addition to The Gates series. The book is very emotional, sweet, funny, romantic, and these two are great together. I look forward to every book in this series."
—Elaine Gray on *Sawyer*

"This book has all the feels and pulls the reader right in. It was wonderful to see how the two of them went from adversaries to respect to falling in love. You won't want to miss their story to see the path they travel and if there is a HEA waiting at the end. There is much more going on here, but hopefully this is enough to convince you that you will not want to miss this one."
~Emily Pennington on *Trey*

www.BOROUGHSPUBLISHINGGROUP.com

BRICK
Copyright © 2021 M. Tasia

ISBN: 978-1-953810-67-0

To my family for their unwavering support.
I love all of you to the moon and back.

ACKNOWLEDGMENTS

To all my readers: Thank you. There's no escaping the truth – without all of you, there wouldn't be me, the author. Your support and kind words has taken me from being a new author who was unsure and panicked to an author with over twenty books under her belt. Okay, I'm still unsure and panicked, but I'm a work in progress. (Takes a sip of wine.)

I love sharing my stories with you and hearing how my characters have touched you and how you've cheered them on, cried with them, and even wanted to knock some sense into a few. Your encouragement has inspired me to continue on my writing journey. All the late nights, missed events, and looming deadlines have been worth it knowing these stories have entertained and stayed with you long after the book is finished.

BRICK

Prologue

The house looked much the same as Brick remembered from childhood, except for the years of rot, infestation, overgrowth, and dirt. They were new unwelcome additions. The large wraparound porch looked ready to crumble if someone dared to step on the boards. Large broken and cracked single-pane windows had long lost their seals and any energy efficiency they might've had. The shutters were hanging by sheer will, at least the ones still attached to the faded and battered exterior.

Brick got out of his truck and stood in the long lane as he tried to wrap his head around the truth: he was the lake house's new owner. His Great Aunt Sophia had passed away two years ago while he was overseas during a tour of duty. She'd left him this place for some unknown reason, and today marked the day he moved in.

He heard animals scurrying underneath the steps as he carefully navigated his way onto the porch, literally tiptoeing to the large ornately carved door. That would be one thing that'd definitely stay once it'd been restored.

He'd enjoyed the time he'd spent at The Gates and had garnered a lot of information from the guys restoring the condo conversion above a swank restaurant in DTLA. Max Connor whose construction company was working the building reno had been a wealth of information and had said he'd come down to Texas and take a look at the lake house if Brick needed any help. Stand-up guys over there in California.

The boards creaked underneath his boots as he pulled out the key and unlocked the back door. The stale air assaulted him, the stench of years of dust layered over everything: a musty reminder the house had been neglected for far too long. Sheets covered most of the items in the living room and dining room, but the kitchen looked the same as when his aunt had been alive.

There was an empty mug sitting beside the old six-cup coffee machine. Newspapers from over two years ago were piled on the counter, and a single chair was pulled back from the kitchen table as if waiting for his great aunt's return. Even her sparkly cane stood leaning against the wall.

It'd crushed him when he couldn't make it back for her funeral. At the time, he was deep behind enemy lines on a mission. She had been so proud when he'd become a Navy Seal, though she didn't like the danger he was sure to encounter on his missions. He well remembered her cheering him on when he walked up to the podium to have his gold trident pinned to his uniform.

He went downstairs first and wandered the rooms in the basement, before returning to the ground, and then went up to the second floor as he tried to develop a plan. What was he going to do with all this room and ten acres of forested waterfront land?

He stopped in the front room with its wall of windows facing Fire Lake. The view was stunning, with large red cedars and oaks framing the calm waters. The sound of water lapping at the shoreline was a melody he'd fallen asleep to more times than he could count.

Brick had spent a lot time in and on the lake, and had caught bass his great aunt had fried it up to perfection. She'd always made a big deal every time he returned with a catch or two. She'd prepare them a special way, which she never shared, and set out the good china even though it was usually only the two of them.

He'd loved visiting Sophia. Even as he grew older, he'd make sure to visit as often as he could. Though he felt sure she understood why he couldn't come stateside while she was sick, he was a long way from forgiving himself for not being there when she needed him. It didn't matter other family members were with her when the end came. He wasn't there, and to this day, he felt his absence was unforgivable.

Brick opened the garden doors and stepped into the waning sunlight. Sophia's prized flower beds were overgrown, and her climbing roses grew wild into the surrounding bushes. The stone birdbath was missing its pedestal, and the garden shed's roof had caved in. The yard hadn't been mowed in years, and all kinds of grasses reached all the way up to his knees.

The more he looked, the more he found things needing fixing, cleaning, cutting, replacing, or exterminating. This was what happened when a building was left to sit without life in it. The same held true for people.

As he neared the water, a chorus of ducks grew louder in the quiet of the twilight descending around him. The rich loamy smell of the earth and water drew him closer, and a patch of bluebonnets stood in vivid contrast to the green surroundings.

Brick could almost hear Sophia telling the younger him to leave the bluebonnets alone after one misguided flower picking session. That was the day he learned the pretty little wild plant was toxic.

Sitting on the sizable rocks at the water's edge, Brick took a minute to get his head on straight. He couldn't keep the house. It was way too big for one person and required too much work to make it livable. He'd already spent a large portion of his life amid destruction. He didn't think he really wanted to take on resurrecting a structure nearing decimation.

He ran his palm over one of the rocks' rough surfaces and felt deep grooves in the underside. Leaning over, he took a closer look and nearly fell off his rock when he found his great aunt's name embedded into the stone. It wasn't professionally done, more like a backyard hammer and chisel job. Had Sophia done that?

As he felt around the rest of the rock, he found more marks and squinted to make out the letters in the last bit of light. *Christopher*. His legal first name. It appeared Sophia chiseled both of them into the rock. There was a month and date inscribed underneath his name. He thought he was seeing things, but he used his fingertip to trace the numbers. Sure enough, it was dated the same month Sophia had been hospitalized. *Damn*. One of her final acts was adding his name, and maybe hers, to ensure they were both at the lake permanently. Surely, she knew she was dying, and the implications of him finding this.

His hand shook as he brushed the engraving one last time before standing and looking back at the house. "Shit. I can't believe I'm going to do this." He took a deep breath and headed toward the house. This could be the beginning of the best decision he'd ever made or the expressway to insanity.

Brick opened the garden doors and stood in the middle of the main floor as he took stock of everything around him.

Home, Sweet Home.

Chapter One

Seriously, if whoever was at his door kept knocking like a caffeinated woodpecker, Brick was going to lose his shit. He'd been up most of the night dancing with his demons and had finally fallen into a deep sleep when the banging started. It didn't matter it was eight in the morning. Nobody should be knocking on his door. Everyone who knew him knew understood why they had to call first. Surprising a retired Navy SEAL wasn't the wisest or healthiest thing someone could do.

He tried ignoring the knocking, assuming whoever it was would fuck off when no one answered. But no, the idiot switched tactics and was now knocking on the garden doors instead of the back door. Did whoever this asshole was have a death wish?

Brick threw his legs over the edge of his mattress, feeling his sore muscles fight his movement. Some old injuries made their presence known early and often. He grabbed a pair of shorts, palmed his 9mm, and stormed out of his bedroom. The same one he'd slept in when he'd visited his great-aunt. While he was admittedly a creature of habit, the real reason he didn't move into the master was the same as why all the other rooms that held Sophia's things hadn't been touched. He didn't want to sort through the remains of her life. Stupid, he knew, but he'd been putting it off for months. Like not doing it would make her death less real.

The floorboards creaked along with his body as he passed by the kitchen and through the living room. By the time he reached the door, he'd worked up a good head of steam, ready to unload on whoever was on the other side. His right hand at side, the 9mm lying against his thigh, he wrapped his hand around the handle, turned it, and peeked through the crack.

"What the hell do you want?" he growled before registering a woman was on the other side. Luckily, he was able to stop himself before carrying through with his intended tirade. He'd been raised right and yelling at women was off the table.

The woman took a step back, but her perfectly painted smile never left her face. She was dressed in a black suit of sorts, with the skirt's hemline way too high and a blouse cut far too low, leaving nothing to the imagination. Her sky-high designer stilettos rounded out the picture, and the vibes she was sending his way didn't scream my car broke down. In truth, she appeared to be sizing him up.

This should be interesting.

"Hello there, I'm looking for a Mr. Christopher Matthews, the owner of this property," she said without missing a beat or a suggestive glance.

"That would be me, ma'am." He was trying to be polite even though her smile turned a bit lecherous as she gave him the once over, her gaze moving across his chest to the small barbell pierced through his right nipple and down his stomach to the bulge in his shorts where she lingered. If that wasn't an invitation, he didn't know what was. Why did he feel like he needed to take a shower? She was so far from his type they weren't on the same radar screen. "How can I help?"

"Oh, it's not what you can do for me. It's what I can do for you," she said as she winked and sidestepped her way into the living room. She dropped her slim leather briefcase onto an old side chair, sending a cloud of dust up and onto her spotless clothing making her cough and desperately try to wipe the dust from her skirt.

"I'm afraid to ask what you mean by that, ma'am." Brick chuckled as he watched her fret over a designer suit costing more than he made in a month.

"Julia," she provided before taking a few steps closer to an old bookshelf covered in tchotchkes and books. Cobwebs stretched from one corner to the next, decorated with old fly carcasses encased in spider silk, waiting for the owner's return. "This place hasn't aged well. You should be happy to know I can take this headache off your hands." She waved her finger in a circle as she grimaced at her surroundings.

Real estate agent. That fit. He honestly wondered when one would show up, considering he now owned ten acres of prime lakefront property. People had approached his great aunt on multiple occasions attempting to buy the lake house, but she'd refused, and he was of the same mind. Once he'd made the decision to stay, he was all in.

"Before you even get started," he said. "I'm not interested in selling." He wanted to make that clear from the get-go.

The woman spun around to look at him, calculating her next steps. "But you haven't heard the offer. It's quite substantial, I assure you."

"It could be billions of dollars. I'm still not interested," Brick said before heading back to the door to lead her out. "Sorry, you wasted your time. Now, if you don't mind, I have a lot to do today." He gestured to the door, and of course, she headed in the opposite direction toward the kitchen.

With a loud huff, he grabbed her briefcase and followed. Maybe he could get her out the back door. Brick doubted she'd heard the word "no" often.

"Why would you want to keep all of this?" She gestured at the broken side window covered in plywood and the water stains on the ceiling. He hadn't gotten around to finishing the roof. It was on the list.

"That's my business. Now it's time for you to go." Even if he wanted to sell, which he didn't, Sophia had loved the place and he was a man of his word. The house was staying in the family.

She didn't miss a beat. Instead, turning around and facing him as she smoothed her manicured red nails down the deep neckline of her blouse. "Is there anything I can do to change your mind, Christopher?"

"The name's Brick," he corrected before handing her the briefcase. "And to answer your question, no. It's time for you to leave."

Her shocked expression would've amused him if she hadn't dodged his attempt to lead her out. Instead, she walked back into the living room and began removing her blouse. What the hell?

"Are you sure about that, Brick?"

He stopped and really looked at the woman. There was something in her eyes that made him pause. "Is this what they teach realtors these days?"

Again, there was a moment when she looked off. Guilty? Brick went ahead and set her briefcase down on the cluttered counter, noticing the initials R and B engraved on the handles. "Look, Julia, put your blouse back on. I'm gay. There's nothing you can do for me."

Her face fell, and she did as he asked as her cheeks turned red. "That's that then."

That was a weird thing to say. He wasn't an asshole and felt the need to ensure she was fine. Okay. He was an asshole at times, but this wasn't one of them.

"What do you mean?" he asked.

She looked at him with a sad expression and said, "Nothing. I'll be looking for a new job tomorrow is all."

Brick gave her the once over. Scrutinizing her and trying to sort through the mixed vibe he was getting. "Is this another ploy to get me to feel sorry for you, 'cause I can assure you, it's not going to work."

Julia did something he hadn't seen coming. She stepped out of her designer heels. "God, how do people wear these things all day?" She was much shorter than he'd originally believed.

Now that she stood barefoot on the old, dusty floor, he saw more of the real woman underneath the bling. "I take it you don't usually dress this way?"

"Hell no."

That caught him off guard. "You're going to have to explain this to me," he said while waving his finger in her direction much like she had at him.

Julia bowed her head and said, "I'm sorry. This whole thing was a mistake." She peeled off one of her fake nails and looked at it ruefully. "I'm lucky I didn't stab myself with these things."

The picture was clearing in Brick's mind with every word she said until he came to his own conclusions. But he needed more. "Do you even own those shoes?"

She didn't even look up. "Rented."

"Outfit?"

"Same."

"Briefcase with initials not matching your first name?"

Her head popped up. "Goodwill. It was an amazing find."

Brick let out a deep breath. "Stay where you are. I'll be right back," he instructed before heading off to Sophia's old bedroom. He grabbed a pair of her old slippers and a clean sheet from the plastic tubs in storage. When he returned, Julia was still standing in place though looking a bit more nervous.

"Don't worry. I wanna make sure you don't end up with a piece of this old floor in your foot. Put these on." He handed over the slippers before going over to the dusty chair and placing the clean sheet over it. "Sit." If the outfit was rented, he now understood why earlier she was frantically trying to clean the dust off. There'd be a dry-cleaning charge for sure.

Brick didn't wait to see if she followed his instructions. He was positive she would. He turned on the electric kettle and set out two clean mugs. "Tea or coffee?"

"Tea, please," she called out, not even sounding like the same woman who'd knocked on his door less than fifteen minutes ago.

He was no damn counselor by a long shot. Hell, he probably needed one himself, but he'd had a sister once before cancer stole her away, and Julia looked like she could use a big brother right now.

While waiting, he glanced outside and noticed there wasn't a car in the driveway and wondered how she got here. Once the water was boiling, he put everything on one of Sophia's serving trays and carried it over to the side table beside Julia's chair. "I've got sugar, but the milk's gone bad. I like my coffee black." He grabbed one of the kitchen table's chairs, spun it around, and sat down with his arms leaning on the back of the chair, looking straight at his guest.

"Spill it." He didn't do coaxing.

Julia took a sip of her tea before answering, undoubtedly deciding how much to tell him. He'd wait as long as it took. "I'm not a real estate agent."

"Then who are you, and why would you come here to buy my property?"

"I'm only the secretary in a real estate office over in Marshall."

"Why would they send you?"

"Because everyone else is either geriatric or male. Huh, little did they know," she laughed without any real joy.

"So, they sent you out knowing I was a single male to do what… seduce me?"

"If necessary."

"And you agreed to this?"

"What choice did I have? I need the job."

"There is no job worth selling yourself for," he said, unable to keep the growl from his voice.

"Said like a single man without a child at home to feed." He heard the venom in her voice and took a mental step back.

"This boss of yours picked you to convince me to sell my land, and if you didn't, you'd be fired?" He wanted the whole truth.

"Jake, yeah. He called me into his office and told me he had some rich buyer for your place, and if I couldn't get you to sell, then I wasn't the type of team player he needed."

"Team player." Brick sneered.

"And because he knows I'm a single mom, I'm the perfect person to threaten. I'm not stupid. There aren't that many decent-paying jobs in Marshall, so the asshole knew I'd be desperate enough to do what he wanted."

"Who's this rich buyer?" Julia rolled her blue eyes, making him wonder how old she was under all that makeup. "How old are you?"

"Twenty-one."

Shit. "And that asshole sent you out here?"

Julia shrugged her shoulders as if being taken advantage of was commonplace. "I don't know who the buyer is, but it must be on the offer I brought. The who didn't matter to me at the time."

"I understand," Brick said before standing and retrieving the briefcase from the kitchen counter. He pulled out a sealed white envelope with gold embossing around the edges and tore it open. The dollar amount meant nothing. It was the gold letterhead that caught his attention."

"Furrow and Son Investments," Brick said as he wracked his brain to remember where he'd seen that name before. "Why do I recognize it. Do you know anything about them?"

Julia faced scrunched up for a moment before her eyes went wide, and she stood. She raced over to the bookshelf and pulled out a stack of envelopes from between two books. "I saw these when I walked by the case earlier," she said as she handed them to Brick."

Every envelope had the same golden design as the one he'd just opened. Brick sat down at the kitchen table and began sorting through the envelopes. A few weren't even opened. Julia came over to help and began pulling the letters out for him to read. All were from the same company, and most were one line only containing a number that he assumed were introductory offers. Brick checked the dates, and they stretched back almost ten years.

"Whoever this is, really wants your property, Brick," Julia said as she handed him the last letter. It read *Name your price.*

Who the hell does that? Some rich asshole with more money than brains, who couldn't take no as an answer and now thought they could move in on Sophia's land now that there was a new owner.

"They have no idea who they're dealing with," Brick snarled, but surprisingly Julia didn't step back at his anger.

"This has been going on for a while," she said as she looked through the letters. "I only started working there a little more than a year ago."

Brick couldn't help his curiosity. "Where's your baby's daddy?"

Julia looked down for a moment before squaring her shoulders and setting her chin. "Gone the moment Sammy was born. It's the two of us now." She had strength in her, that was for sure.

"How did you get here? There's no car in the driveway." She looked panicked for a moment, and Brick quickly put the pieces together. "Did someone drive you out here?"

"Yes. It's a ways from Marshall, and I didn't know if my car would make it."

"Who drove you here?"

Julia quickly looked away and muttered, "Jake."

Brick held back his anger as he'd been trained to do when he was confronted with bad behavior by detestable people who take advantage of those weaker than them. Never let them know what you're thinking or feeling. However, a plan was quickly taking form in his mind. It was time certain individuals learned that their days of lording were done.

"Julia, this is what we're going to do."

***

Once he stepped away from his lake house, the trees and brush were thick. However, the terrain felt familiar as he ghosted through the branches and groundcover without making a sound. Each step was chosen several steps ahead of where he was currently positioned. His senses attuned to his surroundings. Every rustle, scrape, or crack was processed and accounted for.

This felt natural to him, not navigating the world he'd been thrust into after he became a civilian. Dug into mud-filled trenches, camouflaged on mountain tops, buried in the sand—these situations felt more comfortable than having to deal with the endless complications of everyday life. At least with his team, Brick knew someone always had his back. Here, he was on his own, but he'd be damned if he'd allow this abusive Jake person to continue unchecked.

He saw the car sitting off to the side of the dirt road about one hundred yards away from the house. A guy whom he assumed was Jake sat in the driver's seat with his polished cowboy boots resting on the passenger side dashboard. Leaning back, with a black Stetson covering his face as eighties rock blared from the car's speakers.

Getting to within a couple of feet of his prey was simple. The guy would never hear an ambush coming. So sure in his power, this sorry excuse for a man sent a twenty-one-year-old girl in to seduce him into selling his property while the bastard sat out here like a damn pimp.

His anger bubbled below the surface, and Brick couldn't help the growl escaping his throat, a slip that would've gotten him killed in another life. Jake took his hat off his face and looked around, searching, and completely missing the threat only a few feet away.

Footsteps could be heard coming closer, and within a few moments Julia came into sight carrying her precious briefcase while navigating the bumpy path in those awful heels. Brick watched as she walked up to the passenger door and went to open it when Jake locked her out. The passenger window was partially open, and it was easy to hear what they were saying on the quiet backroad. Brick took out his phone and hit record.

"Not so fast, missy," Jake said. "Do you have good news for me?"

"Open the door, Jake," Julia snapped while pulling on the door handle again.

"Not until you tell me what I want to know. If I don't like what I hear, you're walking back to Marshall."

"That's over thirty miles away."

"It'll give you lots of time to break into a new line of work," the asshole said.

Now that Jake was sitting up, Brick could get a better look at him. He looked about average but suspected the good-old-boy had a beer belly hidden behind the car door by the way his button-down shirt bunched up under his chest. His dull brown hair was turning grey at his temples, and his handlebar mustache reached well past his jawline.

Julia rolled her eyes at Jake making Brick smile. "I have good news."

"You slept with him. I knew you would. You look the type."

"How could I not with your threat hovering over my head."

"If you're not a team player, then my real-estate firm will no longer employ you. It's simple as that, and it's not a threat. Now, let me know the good news, and I'll judge whether to unlock the doors.

Brick wanted to climb out of the bushes and scare the shit out of the dick, but he'd stick to the plan as he always did, no matter how repulsed he was or eager to right a wrong.

"I got you a personal meeting with the guy."

"A meeting with Mr. Matthews?"

"Ah-huh. I figured you could use your skills to convince him. I paved the way for you. Oh, he wants to meet the buyer at the same time. Something about getting a feeling for the potential new owner."

"Yes," Jake hissed as he unlocked the door. "You must have fucked him good to get him to agree to this," he cheered before deepening his voice. "Maybe you could show me how you did it." He reached over and ran the palm of his hand along the back of Julia's neck, and for a second, Brick thought he'd have to break cover before she spoke.

"Get your greasy hand off of me," she said before grabbing his forearm and pushing him away. "Touch me again, and I'll cut off your balls and ram them down your throat."

Jake straightened in his seat and turned the key starting the grey sedan. "Geez, you don't have to be violent about it. I mean you spread for one, what's the big deal about spreading for another?"

If he thought she was being violent, Brick had a few things to show him.

The car took off, and he tapped off the recorder, then slid his phone back in his pocket. Then he made his way back the same route he'd come.

This was far from over.

Chapter Two

Brick jumped into the old twelve-foot fishing boat he'd used when he was a kid and grabbed the pull cord, cranking the newly serviced outboard motor. It came sputtering to life after the first few tries bringing a smile to his face. He'd been able to repair it, and frankly, he'd guessed at much of what he'd done. He'd made sure to stow a paddle in the boat alongside his new fishing rod. It was always best to be prepared.

After days of back-breaking work making the lake house watertight, he figured he'd earned a couple of hours off to go out bass fishing like he'd done when Sophia was alive. A fish dinner sounded just about perfect after weeks of hotdogs and hamburgers on the grill. Besides he needed to clear his head before his meeting with the sleazy agent and his buyer. Brick had been running scenarios through his mind ever since his meeting with Julia a week ago, and he needed a brain break from what he knew was coming.

With renewed spirits, he grabbed hold of the tiller and eased away from the dock, which had been recently rebuilt by a couple of college students who'd stayed with him over the summer helping him get the lake house back in shape. He smiled as the boat glided away from shore and headed for open water.

The wind lashed at his face and felt invigorating as he opened up the old 9.9 engine and angled his way out to his favorite fishing hole. He'd always had an affinity for water and had spent many days on the decks of one battleship or another over the years. The water soothed him like nothing ever could. The sun was shining high above, and there wasn't a cloud in the sky—blue as far as the eye could see. The perfect day.

When he approached the small but familiar L-shaped island, he navigated through the rocky outcropping until he reached the sweet spot, a small cove shaded by large oak trees and covered in moss. There had to be more than a couple of fish hanging out in this area that was protected from the hot Texas sun and had an ample supply of minnows to feed from.

He picked his spot, dropped his small anchor, which in reality was a cement-filled milk jug, and threw his line into the water. Brick had found his old fishing box in the remains of the old shed, which had collapsed. He'd rebuilt it, and in so doing, it provided him with the impetus to pull the old boat motor apart to see if it had any life left in it. Now he was here in his old fishing spot waiting for his first nibble like he'd done so many times in years past. He let out a deep breath and relaxed his shoulders.

His life had taken quite a turn since the last time he was out on the lake. He'd fought in wars that were splashed across television screens, and many that never saw the light of day. Retired Navy Seals were far and few between. Making it twenty years doing the shit he'd done wasn't always possible for various reasons. Some did a couple of tours before deciding not to re-up. It was a physically and mentally insane job they did to keep the world safe from the darker sides of reality. Some never made it back from their last mission alive. The SEAL units accounted for the highest percentage of warriors who never made it to retirement.

From infiltrating behind enemy lines in search of their ever-changing targets to stopping the sale of nuclear missiles to those who would like nothing more than to see the west burn, at times it'd been a daily battle keeping the civilian population oblivious of how close they'd come to annihilation.

He'd signed up for the Navy at eighteen and became a SEAL at twenty. They provided him with an education along the way, and that BA allowed him to rise through the ranks. When he turned thirty, he became a Lieutenant and led his own platoon, and by thirty-six, he rose to the rank of Lieutenant Commander before retiring at thirty-eight.

Brick had stashed away every reenlistment bonus, along with all of his hazard pay and most of his salary, as a nest egg for when he got out. He was using that money to repair and rebuild the lake house. So far, it had been working out well, as long as he didn't veer too far from his budget.

Over his twenty years of service, he'd received numerous medals. Pieces of tin decorated with colorful ribbon sat stuffed in a box somewhere. A lot of good that did him now when all he wanted was peace instead of a head crammed full of nightmares that appeared whenever he closed his eyes and the odd time when they were open. Yeah, he'd been diagnosed with PTSD, but what SEAL who'd put in twenty years hadn't? The shit they did, and the secrecy they lived with, wasn't natural, normal or easy to process. Especially for the type of person who became a SEAL. They weren't known for their warm and fuzzies.

A small tug on his fishing line had Brick refocusing his attention to the task at hand. Another nibble had him tightening his hold on the fishing rod. Patience was key, and luckily, he had honed that skill long ago.

The anticipation made the blood pump through his veins a bit faster, and his sight zeroed in on the tip of his rod. At any moment, he'd have the first decent meal since arriving at his new home. Of course, he could have bought fillets at the grocery store, but where was the fun in that? Any moment now—.

The scream of an electric guitar and the booming of a techno beat, along with the roar of some serious horsepower, broke around the edge of the small island seconds before a massive multi-level cabin cruiser came into view. The thick trees must've muffled the noise when they were behind the island. Shit. All hopes of his fresh-catch dinner vanished when the fish decided the worm wasn't worth the trouble.

The beast was only a couple hundred yards away, moving at a pretty healthy clip while the herons and ducks took to the sky in a panic. Brick could easily make out several young women draped all over the deck in their string bikinis while others drank from champagne flutes and danced to the music.

He didn't recognize the older man behind the wheel, but Brick learned all he needed to know when he saw the stern of the boat. The boat was named "Mr. Furrow." He'd bet it was the same Furrow of Furrow and Son Investments. He wondered if the guy knew how big a cliché he was.

The asshole probably had a cottage on the lake. Wouldn't that suck? There was no way in hell that boat could be moored against his or anyone else's docks in the area, the water wasn't deep enough for such a big boat. It'd end up running aground and damaging the hull.

He didn't have to wait long before they were out of sight behind the island's west side, oblivious to his boat, and the lake's speed limits.

His small, dented fishing boat bobbed up and down as the larger boat's wake threatened to swamp him. Waves rolled up over the side of his boat, soaking him, his gear, and his motor. Thankfully he managed to stay afloat with some quick maneuvering and weight distribution.

When he had the boat under control and out of danger he reeled in his line, shook out his gear, and turned around to grab the pull-cord. His day on the water was over. He gave the cord a yank, nearly pulling his shoulder out of its socket in the process when it refused to budge. After several attempts and a quick once over, Brick accepted his fate, grabbed the paddle, and began the long, arduous journey back to the house.

"Fucking Furrow," he grunted. His arms ached, and he hadn't even made it halfway back when another larger fishing boat came along traveling below the speed limit.

"Hey there, we can see you might need some help," an older man in his early seventies said as he brought his boat up alongside him. "Engine trouble?"

Brick threw the paddle into the bow of his boat and flexed his sore hands. "That would be appreciated, sir." He wouldn't be moving his arms right for days.

"No worries, son. We'll get you to shore," he replied as a chocolate lab poked its head over the side of his boat. "I'm Jeff, and this here is Molly."

Stretching out his arm to shake the man's hand. "Brick. I'm happy you two came along. I'm not sure how much further I'd make it rowing."

"I'm sure you would've made it to where you needed to go. You guys don't know the meaning of the words give up." Jeff chuckled as he threw a line over, and Brick went on alert. "Special forces," Jeff continued as he motioned toward Brick's chest. Instinctively he wrapped his hand around his black dog tags.

"Navy SEAL."

Jeff dipped his index finger beneath the worn collar of his shirt and pulled out a set of his silver tags. "Army."

"Well, hell. How am I ever going to live down a ground pounder saved me out here on the water?" Brick scowled.

Jeff smiled wide. "Yep. I'll be sure to mark it down on my damn calendar," he laughed before throwing Brick another towline. "At least I'm not a crayon eater."

After a couple more friendly jabs between Army and Navy, they were almost on their way when Jeff asked, "Where we headin'?"

Brick scanned the horizon and pointed in the direction of the house. "Over in that direction along the peninsula. Big white lake house with the wrap-around porch."

"You talking about Sophia Matthews's old place?" Jeff asked, looking surprised.

It wasn't uncommon in small communities to know everyone living there, and a good deal about their business. "I'm Sophia's great-nephew."

The guy's face lit up like he'd been handed the winning lottery ticket. "You've finally made it back. That's great. Sophia would be over the moon to know you're here taking care of it."

"I'd like to think so." In truth, he still wasn't sure he'd made the right choice, but he'd never turn back now. He'd invested too much time and money to walk away.

As they neared his dock, Brick couldn't help notice the large Furrow cabin cruiser anchored at the far end of the same peninsula his house was on. It was a substantial distance away, but he could make out smaller boats traveling between the cruiser and the partially hidden mansion sitting up on the rocks. It couldn't be.

"If you want some good advice, son, stay away from old man Furrow," Jeff nodded toward the mansion. By the curl of his upper lip and squint of his eyes, Brick knew there was some deep anger behind that look.

"That his place?" Brick asked. "You know him?"

"Yeah, that's one of his homes, and everybody knows him. Whether they want to or not."

"That requires a further breakdown," Brick said as he reached for one of the metal cleats he'd bolted to the dock and pulled the boat closer before tying it to. He'd have to tear the engine down to see if he could fix it again. "What do you mean, want to or not?"

"He's the richest man in the county, and he makes sure everyone is clear on that. Pompous asshole. He used to bug your great-aunt almost monthly to sell her land to him, but she never gave in to the bastard." Jeff looked at Brick in question.

Instead of answering, he asked his own question. "How do you know so much about her?" Brick jumped out of the boat and stood on the dock, looking at Jeff.

"We were friends. When I got out of the service, Sophia became my sounding board of sorts. A confidant when I needed someone to talk to when things got to be too much. She was an incredibly special person, and I owe her a lot."

Brick could see the truth in the man's eyes and relaxed a bit before saying. "I don't intend to sell the property either. Mr. Furrow's has already been in contact."

"The asshole moves pretty fast," Jeff said while shaking his head.

"Well, it's about time someone slowed him down," Brick said, not bothering to hide his grin.

Jeff rubbed Molly's head and said, "Be careful. I've heard stories going back decades about the old man. If you need any help, the guys and I typically hang out over on Jackson pier fishing most days." He reached into his pocket and pulled out his wallet before handing Brick a business card.

"Veteran Counseling?" The words were embossed on the business card in bold print and there was a phone number and email address at the bottom.

Jeff smiled wide. "My way of carrying on her kindness."

"You wanna come up to the house for a beer?" Brick wouldn't mind hearing more stories about his great-aunt.

"Love to, but it'll have to be another time. I have an appointment this afternoon," Jeff said.

"Anytime. It's an open invitation. Thank you for the tow home and the warning."

"We'll take you up on that," Jeff said before backing his boat away from the dock and, with a wave, heading east toward town. Molly's barks carried a long way across the water, and Brick could still hear her when they were out of sight.

He stood for a few moments staring at the mansion in the distance.

It was time for some recon into the Furrow family, and he knew exactly who to call.

Chapter Three

"Father," Roman yelled as he slammed the front door shut behind him. He needed to put a tracker on the man. This shit was getting old fast.

Two scantily clad women giggled from the top of the stairs giving him a direction in which to start searching. Since retiring, his father lived life like a never-ending party while Roman worked his balls into knots as President and CEO of Furrow and Son Investments.

When he wasn't in Dallas working his ass off, he was busy cleaning up after his miscreant father. Stephan Furrow's latest request had him flying in to find out what the hell was going on here in Hill Country.

Roman took the stairs two at a time until he was outside his father's master suite. He didn't bother knocking. Instead, he flung open the door and walked straight in. As he'd surmised, more women mingled in the expansive suite, and he noted the empty champagne bottles as he went toward the brick terrace at the other end of the bedroom.

Again, he wasn't shocked to find multiple women sunbathing in the nude while his father, who was sitting on a large, round daybed, ran his hands over the woman lying beside him. Ever the exhibitionist when it came to women and money, his father had gotten worse in his excess. Age hadn't mellowed him, it empowered him to misbehave worse than when he'd been working.

"Father, we need to talk," Roman stated from the foot of the bed, giving it a kick for good measure to get his point across. "Now." He watched as the flavor of the week extricated herself from the cushions, and with a perfectly plump pout, sashayed inside. His father barely raised his head in acknowledgment. Probably drunk or high. Hell, maybe both.

"You work too much," his father huffed. "Why don't you take Cynthia over there? She'll relieve some of that stress you're carrying."

Roman glanced over at the tall blonde, sizing him up like a piece of meat. He'd checked into each of the women who frequented his father's company and found they were all professionals. Roman would never stand for someone being taken advantage of, but these ladies knew the score and pursued this type of relationship.

"Again, I'm gay, so no thank you. You know, I wouldn't be so stressed if I hadn't come across your latest request." Roman was running out of sympathy for his father, who'd been forced into retirement. Way overdue in Roman's opinion.

"Request? I own and run that company. If I wanted a billion dollars, that shouldn't be a problem."

Here we go. It always started the same way. "You owned, and now I run the company," Roman reminded for the hundredth time. "You receive a monthly stipend that's more than generous."

"Generous? I built that company," Stephan growled.

"Again, no, you didn't. But you did manage to run it into the ground over the past twenty-five years. If I hadn't taken control, there would be no money left for you to spread around like we own a goddamn printing press."

Roman didn't like raising his voice, but his father had lost all sense of reality. "The firm is finally turning around, and what it doesn't need are random requests for three million dollars. What the hell do you need that's worth that much money?"

"Ten acres of waterfront land," his father answered and got that crazy-ass cross between a hawk and a hungry hyena look in his eyes whenever there was something just out of his reach.

"You have over one hundred acres in this area alone. You don't need more land." He had more than he knew how to deal with. It wasn't a new tune.

Dear old dad jackknifed so fast on the daybed that the whole thing moved at least two feet back. "Yes, I do. I've been hunting this property for a decade, and I finally have a meeting with the new owner."

"What's so damn important about this piece of land?" Why did he even ask?

"It's the final holdout keeping me from owning this entire peninsula." His father waved his arms around, reminding Roman of a peacock flashing his feathers.

Roman didn't even bother pointing out that the state-owned park was on the same landmass. It, along with a slew of other truths, wouldn't't've made a difference to his father.

"You mean the Matthews's place on the beginning of the peninsula?" Roman had heard about that property for the past decade or more. The one holdout. "How the hell did you get them to sell?"

"Well, it's not a done deal yet, but I have a meeting with the new owner. The old bird's nephew, Christopher Matthews. I gave him an offer that was quite generous and sweetened the deal a little. Then pow, I get a meeting where I intend to buy that damn property once and for all."

"Sweetened the deal?" Did he want to know?

"Details. All that matters is I've got an in with the owner," Stephan said, and Roman waited for him to rub his hands together like some maniacal cartoon villain.

"When is this meeting?" There was no way it was happening without him.

"Thursday at two," Stephan replied as his eyes turned to slits. "Why?"

Roman thought about it for a moment and decided to let his father play this out. "I'm not releasing the money to you until after that meeting, which I will be attending."

"What the hell? You've never had a problem with my expenses before?" His father struggled to get out of the over cushioned daybed and stand. Roman didn't offer him a hand.

"Well, father, we took the opportunity to go through those many expenses and have concluded that after you tried to buy an elephant when you decided suddenly you wanted to open a private zoo for yourself and your friends, that we'd be keeping a better eye on you."

"We? Who the hell are we?" He crossed his arms over his chest. It wasn't as intimidating as when Roman was a kid.

"Mother and I." He couldn't help the grin.

"How is your mother involved? I divorced that crone years ago." Ever the petulant child, his father didn't realize if his ex was a crone, he was a geezer.

"Yes, as always, you seem to forget that she owns twenty-nine percent of Furrow and Son Investments. Therefore, she has a say and holds a position on the board of directors."

"I own twenty-nine percent. My say matters as well," he countered petulantly.

"Considering, I own forty-two thanks to grandpa, and I agree with her and would vote my shares with her, your say...not so much."

"You're siding with that bitch? Your grandfather would be rolling in his grave to see how you're treating your father. I've given you everything you have."

"Always a pleasure to hear the respect you show my mother who loves and cares for me. Unpaid, *I*'ve worked my ass off for you for more years than I choose to count. I have no doubt, I've paid with interest whatever debt you think I owe you." Aside from the obvious recurring argument, Roman was angry his grandfather had been brought into it this time. "As for grandpa, he knew what he was doing when he left me his shares. He was the person who built the company from the ground up."

"I'm your father."

"Yes, that's what it says on the birth certificate. Now back to the subject at hand. No money if I can't be part of the negotiations." That may sound cruel, but was absolutely necessary. Stephan would use emotional blackmail every time he demanded something, and at this point in Roman's life, such antics held no sway over him. Not anymore.

"One of these days, you're not going to be so high and mighty," he warned.

"I don't want to be this way, but you're forcing me to reign you in. Your spending has nearly sent the company into receivership. Hell, do you think it's my life's ambition to argue with you over your mercurial whims? Fuck, when did I become the parent?" Roman was past frustrated and tired.

He'd taken the red eye to make it from Dallas after late meetings only to drive out here from the Austin airport to find his father lounging in the sun with his female entourage. He didn't want to be the adult in their relationship, but he'd been forced into the position by his father's erratic behavior.

"I'll be staying until the meeting," he said and turned his back on his father. He was heading for the office to get in touch with his assistant. She'd have to rearrange the next couple of days of his schedule where he'd continue to work from Fire Lake until this matter was resolved.

He found his luggage and briefcase sitting at the bottom of the stairs. Gerard, his father's butler, must have had them brought in. The man was a saint, and Roman couldn't figure out why he remained working for his father. He was loyal to his own detriment.

Roman grabbed his briefcase and headed into the office at the end of the hallway. The room was spotless and looked hardly used, which wasn't surprising. His father wasn't much of an office type.

This was going to be a long week.

***

The hum of a boat's engine caught Brick's attention. It was getting closer by the minute, bringing him out from under the house where he was busy replacing the older pipes. He wiped the dirt from his t-shirt and jeans while scanning the horizon to get a better look at who was headed his way.

He knew by the sound of the engine that it wasn't Jeff and Molly, and, thankfully it wasn't Furrow. So, who was the new arrival? He'd never been so popular. He didn't like it. The boat slowed as it neared his dock, and he searched the twenty-two-foot bowrider finding only the driver on board.

"Ah fuck," Brick groaned and began walking toward the dock. His new guest stopped roughly twenty feet from him and waited.

Brick stood at the end of the dock and crossed his arms. "Whatcha doing here, Fletcher?"

The big man smiled wide. "By the sounds of things, you could use a little help out here."

Leave it to the best damn extraction man he'd ever known to show up randomly. "Where did you hear that, and what the hell happened to call first?"

"Spence called me, and I was worried you'd say no." The guy had always been honest and to the point.

"I should've known Spence couldn't keep his mouth shut."

"Permission to come ashore, Lieutenant Commander." The formal nature didn't surprise him. Some habits die hard.

"I know I'm going to regret this," Brick said, shaking his head. "Permission granted."

"Yee-haw," Fletcher hollered, gunned his engine, and spun around in a circle before bringing the boat up to the dock to be moored. "Good to see you again, sir." He saluted as he jumped out of the boat and stood at attention.

Brick couldn't contain his smile. "At ease. We're not in a combat situation anymore, Seaman Fletcher, call me Brick."

"Yes, sir," he said while looking around. "You've got yourself a nice place here, S-Brick."

"It's coming along. How long you been here, and where'd you get the boat?"

"Half a day to get a lay of the land, and I bought it from a boat dealership over in Marshall."

"And your car?"

"Rental dropped off."

"Come on. You've got to be hungry. I'll throw some burgers on the barbeque. Go grab a couple of beers from the kitchen," Brick instructed as he went over to the water tap sticking out from the side of the house. He turned it on and put his dirt-covered head under the cold stream to clean up a bit before cooking.

By the time he'd finished, Fletcher had brought out the burgers, buns, and beers. Perfect. Brick got the grill going and set the burgers on the grates to cook. He twisted the cap on his beer and took a long pull before joining his guest sitting at the old patio table. Fletch stared unmoving out onto the lake, his beer unopened. Something was up, and it had nothing to do with the lake house.

"What did Spence have to say to get you out here so fast?"

Fletch jolted out of his thoughts, grabbed hold of his beer, and opened it. "He said some guy he was looking into was pressuring you to sell your great-aunt's lake house."

Brick could feel there was more to this than Fletch was letting on, but he was patient. "Yeah, and I've found more offers from this dude scattered around the house trying to buy it from Sophia, but she'd refused. My guess is he thinks he can swoop in and take it now that she's passed on."

"Won't he be in for a surprise," Fletch chuckled deep in his large chest. "Maybe instead of a quick visit, I should stick around for a bit in case this dude doesn't take no for an answer and you need back up."

Brick didn't miss the hopeful expression on his face. "You're welcome to stay, buddy, no questions asked." Hell, he'd needed a place to hunker down a time or two.

"I can help you fix the place up," Fletch offered.

"Damn straight, you will," he huffed with a bit more force than necessary. "I'm not running no bed and breakfast bullshit around here. You stay, you work."

Stress melted from Fletch's face as he finally gulped his beer. "Thank you, sir." His smile widened as they both sat back, listening to the flow of the water and the sizzle of the grill for a few moments.

Spence was an old friend and an information specialist. He'd sent Brick a report this morning about one Stephan Julius Furrow, and it painted a vastly different picture of the man who seemed to have the world by the short and curlies. He wasn't the all-powerful businessman he portrayed himself to be with his multimillion-dollar offer, the mansion on the hill, and the shiny boat that nearly sank Brick. Apparently, Furrow had been forced out by the board of directors after years of mismanagement and reckless spending.

"I'll give you the rundown of events thus far so you can be up to speed and ready for the meeting coming up," Brick stated. If Fletch was going to stay, he had to know the details. From Julia's clandestine visit, finding all the other offers, and the boat incident, he didn't leave anything out.

"The bastard tried to force a single mother into prostituting herself," Fletch growled, and his eyes went dark. "Mansion on the hill over there, you said."

"Don't go getting any ideas. This is all going to be handled on the up and up. If I intend to live in this area, I can't be taking matters into my own hands."

"Fine," Fletch grumbled, but didn't argue. "What's the plan?"

It was Brick's turn to smile.

Chapter Four

After days of working remotely, Roman was ready to get back to his office and away from his father. The man had no sense of reality or decency. Roman couldn't count on two hands how many times he'd found his father with one or more of his entourage in various forms of undress all over the house.

He presumed there was a stash of Viagra hidden somewhere in this house because there was no way in hell a man of seventy-three with a body compromised by excess and gluttony could keep that up.

After the meeting this afternoon, Roman intended to drive back to Austin and catch the first flight out to Dallas before the late afternoon thunderstorms arrived. He closed his laptop and sat staring out the window in the direction of the Matthews's house, wondering what was next on his father's agenda. He could remember his parents arguing about that property on more than one occasion.

Mother wanted his father to stop harassing the woman who lived there with his incessant offers to purchase the land. However, once Stephan Furrow got his mind set on something, he was as relentless as they came. Roman considered allowing the purchase to go through but knew it wouldn't satisfy his father and slow his outrageous demands. He doubted anything would dial down his father's antics.

The door flew open, and the man of the hour walked in. "It's time to go. Are you ready?"

He didn't even bother to comment on the fact that his father hadn't knocked. He'd learned long ago that no one and nothing could make Stephan Furrow behave like a decent human being. Case in point, forcing the maid to reclean areas around the house multiple times daily as he carried on like a horny teenager without a concern for anyone or anything but himself.

"Let's get this over with," Roman huffed as he stood from behind the desk. He reached for his dark blue suit jacket and slid it on before grabbing his tablet. "Tell me now if you intend to throw in any surprises."

"Me, never. It's a straightforward purchase," Stephan assured, leading the way to the front door.

"I'll be the judge of that." Roman had seen his father at work when he wanted something. This wasn't going to be as easy as a simple land purchase. Not if his father was involved.

Gerard was waiting outside with the back door of the black Cadillac SUV open so his father could take his seat in the back. Stephan was all but bouncing in his seat with excitement at the thought of completing a purchase he'd been chasing for years. Roman doubted the man had looked this happy at his birth, but he couldn't help but feel grateful for his father's maniacal giddiness. The man wasn't happy often.

"Wait until you see it. Of course, we'll have to tear down that old wreck of a house first thing and level the land, but it's perfect for my new helipad project."

And just like that, the gratitude floated away like ash on the wind. "That's what you intend to do with the property. Store your helicopters on it?"

"I certainly don't want them close to my house. Damn things are far too noisy. We'll have to cut down most of the old forest in the surrounding area, but it's worth it." Stephan sat back smugly and looked out the window at all he owned.

Before Roman had a chance to formulate a response to his father's asinine idea, the vehicle began slowing down and turning into the laneway of the Matthews's residence. He immediately noticed the skid of new lumber off to the side of the house and what looked like a recently repaired roof.

"You positive he wants to sell?" Roman asked.

"I got the meeting. Once I work on him a little, getting the guy to sign on the dotted line should be easy. That old bird thought she'd won." Stephan raised his arms like he was cheering as they neared the house. "Look at me now," he growled while looking up as if talking directly to Sophia in the heavens.

Gerard stopped the SUV and placed it in park before getting out to open Stephan's door. Roman didn't work that way. He exited on the opposite side under his own steam. He could understand a driver in the city because parking was a nightmare. But here it was ostentatious and an intentional fuck you, look at me, I'm rich.

A boat was tied to a new dock, furthering Roman's belief that a sale was not imminent, but his father was blind to the obvious renovations happening all around them. Two men came out of the house as another vehicle pulled in behind their SUV. Magnetic signs were stuck to the doors for some real estate firm out of Marshall. Made sense.

The men stopped roughly ten feet away from them, and Roman assumed one had to be the owner. The man on the left was slightly bigger, red-haired, wearing a t-shirt that read NAVY and was sporting black dog tags. The other man looked military as well. His hair shaved short on the sides and longer on the top, sharp cheekbones, and chiseled, tattoo-covered muscles strained under his white shirt. The outline of another set of dog tags confirmed his suspicions.

The other two who came from the real estate office joined them. The pot-bellied man fell all over himself, shaking his father's hand while a young woman in a pantsuit rolled her eyes.

"Mr. Furrow, it's an honor to see you again, sir," the man gushed.

"Yes, Jake, I'm sure it is," Stephan said as he wiped the palm of his hand on Jake's shirt after shaking his hand.

This time Roman rolled his eyes, catching the tattooed man's attention. Those dark eyes pierced right through him, making Roman feel unsettled and a bit excited at the same time. What the hell? This was not the time or place to be thinking those thoughts. Christ, he needed to get laid when he got back to Dallas.

"This here is Christopher Matthews, Sophia's great-nephew," Jake continued with introductions as he pointed at the man staring at Roman.

"Brick," he said without taking his eyes off Roman. "Call me Brick."

"How charming," Stephan delivered the words with a healthy dose of disdain. "I was sorry to hear about your great-aunt's death." Brick's nod was his only response, and Roman could see the distaste in the curl of his lip. If Stephan noticed, he didn't let it show as he carried on undaunted. "So, let's get on with this."

Jake jumped into action like any good lackie, taking a briefcase from the young lady Roman assumed was his assistant and rifling through it. "I have the paperwork ready to be signed. We simply need to add the selling price, and I can have them filed before the end of the day."

"The offer stands at two million," Stephan stated. "What will it take for you to sign that contract? I'm sure you're anxious to get on with your life without being dragged down by this," he said while waving his arms at the old house, "eye-sore. Just give me a number, and you'll never have to worry about a leaky roof, rusty pipes, or scavengers wandering through the kitchen."

"Who's he?" Brick asked without answering the question, pointing straight at Roman. "Your lawyer?"

Stephan gave Roman a side glance before saying, "No one. Just my son, Roman, being an asshole."

He wasn't surprised by his father's words. He'd heard worse over the years. Brick raised his eyebrow and squinted at his father but covered it quickly. You had to read people's reactions in business, and Roman was one of the best at it.

"This is Fletcher, a friend and former teammate," he provided even though Stephan hadn't asked. Roman nodded at the big man in greeting. "So we know who's all in attendance.

"Would you prefer we talk privately?" Stephan asked, jumping at the opportunity to ditch Roman. "I can have them leave."

"Nice try, old man, but I'm not going anywhere," Roman stated. "Your days of wheeling and dealing behind closed doors are over. You want this land, then everything is above board. No secret deals."

Stephan looked like he wanted to explode. Roman thought it was a fair trade for the "no one" comment. Jake looked confused, perhaps realizing who was truly in charge, while his assistant looked shocked, but Brick eyed him shrewdly. Nothing got past this guy.

"Above board? Really?" Brick asked in what could only be described as leashed anger. "Is that what you call the other day when you sent Jake's assistant, Julia, out here?"

Roman couldn't help his groan. "What the hell did you do this time?" As they frequently did when his father was involved, things were going south, rapidly. He could feel it but was helpless to stop it. His father had fucked him over again.

***

Brick was done playing nice, but there was an outlier in this situation, and his name was Roman. Of course, the information he received from Spence included a bio on the son, but he hadn't expected the man to be a part of this meeting. The animosity between the elder and younger Furrow was obvious, but what it meant for the current situation was a wildcard, and Brick didn't do wildcards. He made plans based on facts, and the facts here were murky.

He considered whether the younger Furrow had anything to do with his father's crazy ass scheme and if he'd been part of the harassment Sophia endured with the constant offers. Then there was the matter of sending out Julia to trade sex for a meeting.

"Julia," he said, and the young woman walked to stand by Brick's side. She took a laptop from the briefcase and tossed her boss's bag to the ground, giving it a little kick for good measure before opening the screen and facing it to the Furrows and their greasy real estate agent.

"What are you doing?" Jake growled. "Get back over here or you're fired."

"Don't worry, Jake," Julia laughed. "I quit. I've received a much better offer."

Brick watched Roman carefully for any recognition of what was going on as he hit the play button bringing the screen to life. "This what you Furrows consider above board?"

The sound of music coming from Jake's car in the video had the real-estate agent turning an appropriate shade of red. As the video played out, Brick watched two vastly different reactions from father and son. While Stephan looked bored, as if watching a young woman being pimped out wasn't even a blip on his radar, Roman's face was flush with anger and disgust. His blue eyes were nothing more than slits, his full lips now a sharp slash across his mottled face.

Either the man was an Oscar-winning actor, or he wasn't part of the original plan. Brick would wait and see before making a decision.

When Jake tried to make a move on Julia in the recording, the young woman visibly shook, causing Brick to lay a protective hand on her shoulder. They'd be talking later about her new position here at the lake house and how she was coping with everything that'd happened.

Brick needed the extra help with his great-aunt belongings, he needed someone to go through all the paperwork piled up almost everywhere. He hoped Julia could make sense of it all.

When the video stopped, Brick was cut off from speaking by a stone-faced Roman. "Get in the SUV."

Stephan turned to look at Roman and asked. "What?"

"Get in the damn vehicle, now," Roman growled. His hands were fists, and he looked ready to deck his father.

"Well, this is taking an interesting turn," Fletch said while watching the show and Brick had to agree. The bastard's son had highjacked their plan. "I had a damn speech ready and all."

"A speech?" Brick asked the typically quiet man.

Fletch grinned. "Maybe it was more like threats chained together."

That made sense. Brick had a few choice words to say himself.

"You're too soft. Business is business," Stephan huffed as if scolding a child. "When will you learn?"

"Is that what you meant by sweetening the pot?" Roman's voice had risen several octaves.

"It worked. She slept with him, and here we are having a meeting." As if the results justified the means.

"Correction, asshole. I didn't sleep with him. Brick is gay," Julia hissed. "He's the first person to treat me decently."

Though Brick wasn't one to flash around his sexuality, he wasn't ashamed about who he was, so he confirmed her statement. "What I wanted was to look into the eyes of the scum who forced a twenty-one-year-old to have sex in exchange for a meeting. Now that I have, all I see is a pathetic old man desperate to flex whatever power he has left on people who have no other choice but to listen. You're disgusting."

"Pathetic?" Stephan hissed. "How dare you? Maybe I should have sent Roman over since you both are a little light in the loafers."

"How dare *you*," Roman's voice shook with anger, his veins bulged from his forehead, making Brick worry the guy was going to stroke out. "Let's go. You will leave these people and their land alone, or there will be repercussions you're not going to like."

"Are you threatening me? I'm your father, boy. Show some loyalty." Looked like Stephan was beginning to worry.

"You're one to talk. Now move," Roman ordered before pointing at Jake. "You're done here. But trust me when I say I'm not done with you."

Jake's face went white, and he quickly walked to his car and drove away. Brick watched as Stephan finally acquiesced and returned to his vehicle as the younger Furrow walked to them. Fletch went on alert.

"Easy, let's see what he has to say," Brick stated.

Brick noticed Roman Furrow seemed tired. Spence had laid out the ownership of Furrow and Son Investments, and Brick was shocked to learn Stephan wasn't the principal owner or CEO of the company. He owned twenty-nine percent of the company and Roman owned forty-two, thanks to his late grandfather, and the remaining twenty-nine percent was owned by Stephan's ex-wife, Roman's mother, who sat on the board of directors.

The old bastard had been forced into retirement, but it was obvious Stephan Furrow wasn't fading away as the Board had hoped. Spence had dug up several emails between board members discussing repeated attempts at forcing the former CEO to remain a silent shareholder. Now that Brick had met the guy, he could understand why people didn't want to deal with him.

Roman stopped a few feet in front of Brick, Fletch, and Julia. His handsome face was drawn and pensive. "I'm truly sorry for what my father has done to Sophia and all of you." He looked down at Julia before continuing. "I'm especially sorry for everything you've gone through. Don't worry about the job. I'll make sure your wage continues. No one should ever have to be put into the situation they did to you."

"Pay off?" Fletch countered. "Hush money."

Roman let out a deep breath, and his shoulder sank. "No, I don't operate like my father." He pulled out a business card and handed it to Julia. "You are free to bring an action against your former boss and Stephan Furrow. However, the company was unaware of his actions and did not and does not condone his behavior."

"In other words, you're all for suing Jake and your father, but will fight if the company is brought into this," Brick huffed, unimpressed.

"In a nutshell, yes. I've spent many years saving the company from his mismanagement, and from the specter of Stephan Furrow. I will defend it based on facts. I, as the CEO and the other board members, would never condone, let alone stand idly by while Stephan Furrow made such plans. You need to know, he's not an employee or an officer of the company. He is not our agent in any way. He owns a percentage of the company, that's all. What he did with..." he shook his head, "her former boss, he did on his own. Feel free to go after him personally."

"I didn't plan on suing, but the extra pay would help me and my son find a better place to live," Julia said quietly.

"You have a son?" Roman asked, turning his face up as if trying to get ahold of himself before speaking again.

"Yes. Sammy. He's five."

"The bastard knew this and used it against you. It will never happen again." Roman's eyes laid the man bare, and Brick was surprised by what he saw. Pain.

"Damn straight it won't be," Brick warned anyway. If the younger Furrow wanted to play nice, then he could hold off litigation for now. However, if this turned out to be another trick and the son was as dirty as the father, all bets were off.

"Again, I am sorry for everything my father has done, and I promise you if he tries anything from this point forward, you call me, and I will deal with him," Roman said.

If this was a play, Brick would make the man pay just like his father. Roman held out his hand, and since Brick wasn't a dick, he took it and shook to the plan. He wasn't prepared for the zing of recognition and attraction shooting up his arm when they touched, and he quickly filed it away as deep as possible. This wasn't the time or place for that shit.

"We'll be in touch," Brick said before releasing Roman's hand because they both knew Stephan wasn't going to give up.

Roman sucked in a deep breath and nodded before turning back to the SUV. Strangely, Brick felt the loss of those blue eyes the moment they were no longer directed at him. The three watched as the SUV backed out of the laneway and drove away.

"Okay, what the hell happened?" Fletch huffed. "I was ready for the smackdown."

"Why waste the energy when there was someone else already doing it?" Brick asked. "Strategy, buddy."

"True," Julia agreed. "I was surprised the son was pissed off."

"If he wasn't faking," Fletch added. "It could all be so we don't sue their asses off and go public with it."

"He'd have to be one hell of an actor," Julia said. "We wouldn't go public with this right? I can't live with people knowing what I came out here to do."

Brick wrapped his arm around her shoulder and said, "We would never do anything that caused you harm. We'll keep an eye on them. Trust is earned, so we'll wait and see about the son. Now let's get this day started. Fletch will give you a ride back to Marshall in my truck to collect your things from the office and to have a look at your car. If you're going to be driving out here on the regular, you have to have a safe vehicle."

"Thanks," Julia said but still looked unsure.

"Spill it?"

"Do you think I'm wrong for accepting pay for a job I'm no longer doing?"

"Hell no," Fletch shouted, making her smile.

"You need to decide that for yourself. As for me, I think you've earned it as severance pay for all the shit Jake put you through. But you're the one who has to live with it in the end. If you need a place to live, we can help with that. You don't have to take it."

Julia nodded her head. "Thanks, I'll think about it before deciding."

"Good," Brick said. "Now, let's salvage what's left of the day."

Chapter Five

Brick watched him struggle from the safety of the forest. Sheets of rain poured from the dark sky as lightning lit up the muddy road every so often. Earlier, he'd thought he'd heard something coming down the road, and when a car didn't pass by, he came out to investigate. He found Roman Furrow wielding a lug wrench, trying to change his blown tire on the side of the narrow road.

He was a good distance from his father's house, closer to Brick's in truth. Roman was wearing the same clothes he'd worn that morning, minus the suit jacket. His now soaked white dress shirt clung to his muscled arms and broad chest, both having been hidden under the suit jacket.

Brick knew he was an asshole for sitting back and watching as the guy struggled, but he didn't give a shit if the rich CEO had to get a little dirty. What surprised him was that the guy hadn't called for help and waited in the car until some poor schmuck came out to change the tire.

Brick admitted he was fascinated by Roman and his relationship with his father. He'd sounded like he was on the up and up, but nothing was ever a guarantee. Maybe his behavior was a way of getting out of trouble when his father went too far. Wouldn't want to tarnish the Furrow name, especially after forcing Dad out of the company.

The rain flowed down Brick's face, but he hardly noticed. These situations and conditions were more home to him than anywhere else. He'd once waited more than a week in a Columbian jungle for his target to appear. This was a cakewalk.

Roman cheered when he finally managed to get the tire off the rental car with the slippery lug wrench, but when he went to the trunk and pulled out the spare tire, his face dropped. He set the tire on the ground, and Brick watched as it sank into the mud, flat as a pancake. That sucked.

With the lug wrench in his hand, Roman looked to the skies and shouted his frustration until his voice went hoarse from the effort. Brick watched but was no longer willing to stay uninvolved. He pulled out his phone to call a tow truck to help, but seconds before turning his phone on, a bolt of lightning struck an electric pole a couple of miles down the road.

Okay, it was no longer safe out here, so he broke cover and came out onto the road a few feet from Roman.

"You might want to put that big piece of metal back into the trunk before you kill the both of us." Brick spoke calmly, but he still made Roman jump.

"Shit," Roman hollered. "Where the hell did you come from?"

"California originally."

After a few seconds, Roman dropped the lug wrench lightning rod, making Brick breathe a bit easier.

"How long were you in there watching me?" Roman pointed back into the forest.

"A while. Let's go," Brick said before turning around and walking back into the bush.

"Wait, what? Go where?"

"Back to my house. You're welcome to come along, or you can stay out here and try your luck. It's up to you, but I'm leaving." Brick didn't bother turning around, knowing Roman had enough self-preservation instincts to follow.

When branches cracked behind him, Brick had his answer. He kept the pace slow and easy because he was certain Mr. CEO hadn't been out bushwhacking before today. He heard a few hisses and one ouch but not one complaint, honestly shocking Brick.

Roughly thirty minutes later, the brush thinned, and they came out into his front yard. He could see Fletch standing by the bay window watching for his return. Team members until the end. Brick doubted his friend would've waited much longer if Brick hadn't gotten his ass back here.

By the lit candles and lamps, he figured the electricity must've gotten knocked out with the lightning strike. He'd have to check the fuses when he had a chance, but first, he had to take his guest inside and arrange for a tow truck to come out. Brick stopped when he reached the porch and turned to look at Roman.

"I don't want any shit going down in my house, understand?"

Roman looked a bit worse for the wear after their trek through the trees and brush. Maybe he should have taken it easier on him.

"I understand and thank you for any assistance you can render." Roman seemed sincere, and Brick noticed his hands were shaking.

"Come on in. I'll get you something dry to put on."

Fletch was waiting at the door when they stepped inside. "What the hell happened to him?"

"Flat tire," Brick stated. "There's a tow truck and garage in Marshall. Look 'em up and get 'em out here as quickly as possible." The less time he had to spend with the enemy's son, the better. The man brought out the wrong emotions, and while he couldn't deny the attraction, he was stronger than his base desires.

"On it," Fletch said as he walked a few feet away to grab his phone.

Brick pointed to a closed door. "That's the head. You can get dried up in there while I get you some clothes."

"Thank you," Roman said as he took off his muddy shoes. "I appreciate the help."

Those damn blue eyes looked tired and sad, and all Brick wanted to do was wrap the guy up and protect him. *What the hell is wrong with me?*

He turned away and headed to his bedroom before he did something he'd regret. Grabbing a newer pair of track pants, a t-shirt, and socks, Brick brought the clothes out to the living room and knocked on the bathroom door.

"Yes?"

"I've got dry clothes for you," Brick said, and the door opened, revealing a mostly naked Roman standing in only his boxer briefs. He immediately noticed the red and angry gashes on the guy's arms and shins, as well as older scars. "We'll bandage you up after you put on warmer clothes. Roman looked at him oddly but nodded his head before shutting the door.

He'll be gone soon. He'll be gone soon.

Fletch was on the phone, and Brick went in search of the first aid kit. They may not have all the trappings of the big house on the hill, but they had a well-stocked first aid kit. A Persian rug might save your life in an emergency, but the situations where it would apply were nominal.

By the time he got back to the kitchen, Fletch was off the phone and looking less than impressed.

"What's wrong?"

"They can't get a tow truck out here 'til morning," he grumbled. "The storm's got them hunkered down."

"Of course, they are." Brick knew he was going to regret getting involved. "He'll have to stay the night."

"Great," Fletch growled, not even trying to hide his opinion on that.

"What's great?" Roman asked as he joined them in the kitchen.

Brick would be lying if he said the sight of Roman wearing his clothing didn't do something to him, but he pushed it down. "You'll have to stay the night. The tow truck won't be coming out until morning."

Fletch grinned then said, "Or you could call your father to send someone to get you.

Without missing a beat, Roman said, "Stephan would more likely send someone to run me over on the side of the road."

That statement tracked with what Brick had witness earlier today. The two were not your close buddies-father-son duo. "Why do you call him Stephan instead of father?"

"When I was young, he trained me to call him Stephan when people were around because he said calling him dad made him seem too old," Roman explained without emotion. "Now, I switch back and forth between the two without even noticing it."

"Sit there," Brick ordered while pointing at the closest kitchen chair. He didn't want to examine the anger he felt at Roman's story. Who does that to a kid?

Roman complied immediately, shocking Brick. He'd expected a comment or outright refusal.

"Fletch, can you put on the kettle while I look over his wounds?"

"Sure," his friend huffed before storming over to the counter.

"Your friend doesn't want me here, and I don't blame him," Roman said. "Hell, other people would've left me on the roadside."

"I was tempted," Brick confessed while pulling bandages, alcohol wipes, and antiseptic ointment out of the kit. Instead of frowning, the corners of Roman's lips twitch up.

"I'm certain you were, but I'm grateful you didn't."

"Let's have a look at your arms, and then we'll check your legs. You can get an infection if you don't clean them out properly."

"I'm not going to like this, am I?"

"You might not, but I will," Brick grinned before taking a look at three abrasions on Roman's right arm. He cleaned each one thoroughly before applying the antiseptic and bandages. His patient only hissed twice when he applied the alcohol.

He moved on to the left arm and decided this might be the best and only time he had at getting a few answers.

"You and your father have an interesting relationship."

"You mean strained and unhealthy." Roman gave him a withering look. "We're not close."

"Has it always been like that?" What a way to live.

"No. Not as bad as it is now he's retired."

"Forced retirement," Fletch said as he set three coffees on the table, along with milk and sugar, "you mean to say."

Roman looked up at Fletch and smiled. "Ousted in all due haste. You've done your homework, I see. I would've expected nothing less from former military personnel. Before passing on, my grandfather transferred his shares of Furrow and Son to me instead of my father, giving me control and the yoke around my neck."

"Leg," Brick motioned for Roman's left leg before asking another question. "Your father is persistent. I'll give him that."

"He's a bully, plain and simple," Roman stated.

"Exactly," Fletch huffed before taking a drink of his coffee. "What makes you any different?"

Roman's smile never wavered. "Nothing I say will make you view me differently than my father. You're not the first, and you won't be the last person I find myself apologizing to in my life. First, it was to my friends who dared to laugh in the nineteenth-century European art gallery on a trip to the Dallas Museum of Art and had to sit through an hour-long lecture on civilized behavior. Another time, to my university president for Stephan's decision to buy a yacht instead of funding the library's new wing as he had promised. As the new head of Furrow's, I find myself apologizing to all the people he's screwed over in the past twenty-five years. The truth, I despise him for what he's done to a business built on my grandfather's back. For allowing the Furrow name to be dragged through the mud while he vacationed in Paris or attended film festivals on the Riviera." He stopped to rub his eyes, no doubt as exhausted as he looked. "Listen, I know you have every reason not to trust me after what he did, but all I'm asking for is a chance to prove I'm not my father."

Fletch leaned back in his chair, lowering his aggression slightly. "I'll wait and see."

"Understood, thank you."

Roman looked over at Brick, who was about finished bandaging his final scrapes. While he'd been cleaning the wounds, he couldn't help but take a second look at a few scars on his body, some old, but others quite new.

"We'll see if you're a man of your word," Brick agreed with Fletch on how to handle this, making Roman smile even wider, which delivered a sucker punch to Brick's stomach. He had to think of something else. "Where'd you get these scars?"

Roman's head whipped back at the sudden change in topics. "Accidents mainly. I've been having a run of bad luck off and on these past few years. Nothing really, sometimes I feel like I could trip over my own two feet. The rental car getting a flat is merely a continuation of that."

Fletch looked at Brick as their guest took a drink of his coffee. More information was required.

"Like what kinda accidents," Fletch asked as casually as the big dude could.

"Hmm," Roman's eyes squinted as he thought. "Stupid things, really." He lifted his shirt to reveal a healed scar along his ribs. "This one's from running into a bike courier on the sidewalk outside my office. And this one," Roman pulled up his pant leg to reveal one of the more recent scars on his thigh Brick was concerned about, "I was out biking and a car got too close, so I ended up sideswiping a parked car. I should've been paying closer attention or maybe I should stay away from bikes altogether."

Brick reached for his coffee and took a long drink of the bitter goodness. Black was the only way to drink it. His curiosity now peeked, he needed more. "Was the courier hurt?"

Roman lowered his pant leg and said, "I don't know, he kept going. I honestly didn't expect for the dude to hang around. He was riding on the sidewalk."

"And the car that forced you into parked vehicles on the side of the road?"

"Police didn't find him," Roman answered and looked between the two of them. "Why are you asking so many questions?"

"It's odd," Brick noted.

"Odd? Not for the city. Dallas is among the top places for bicycle crashes and fatalities, or at least according to the investigating officer it is."

"I guess it makes sense," Brick said. "You stay away from bikes, and you'll be fine."

Fletch looked at him oddly, but Brick waved him off. They would talk later. Now it was time to call it a night. "I'll show you where you'll sleep tonight."

Roman's eyes were becoming slits as he struggled to stay awake while nodding his agreement. Brick stood and led him to the bedroom beside his own, it was a guest room in Sophia's days, and the bathroom serviced both rooms. Putting him there had nothing to do with wanting him close by.

"Here you go," he said as he pointed to the closed door and handed him a flashlight. "We'll deal with your car in the morning."

Roman looked at him with humility. "Thank you for saving me out there. I know you don't want me here, and I understand why, but I'm glad for your help all the same."

He opened the door and went inside before Brick could answer. Probably for the best. He didn't know how to respond. You're welcome seemed too plain for the moment and saying more was out of the question.

Brick growled for letting himself get distracted and turned back to the kitchen where Fletch waited. "So, tell me you don't believe he's a statistic on some chart."

"I'll get Spence to look into it. I thought you didn't like the guy, so why should you care if these were truly accidents?" Brick couldn't help the smile on his face. Fletch was a big softy who covered it up with his gruff attitude and big body.

"I don't want the guy dead or anything. That doesn't mean I want to be friends. Besides, it's you who wants to get cozy with the enemy."

Brick had thought he'd kept a lid on his emotions. "What makes you think that?"

"I've known you for over six years, and not once have you offered to dress my wounds. Typically, you tossed the med-kit at my head."

"It was the right thing to do, and you're trained how to dress a wound properly."

"Yeah, keep telling yourself that," Fetch laughed. "You reaching out to Spence tonight?"

"Yep. If something's going on, I wanna know about it." Brick had a bad feeling about this. There was no way he could let it be, especially knowing about the acrimony between Roman and his piece-of-shit father.

"Good. See ya in the morning," Fletch said as he grabbed a bottle of water from the fridge and headed for his room. "Make sure to blow out the candles before calling it a night."

"Yes, mother hen." Fletcher would never change. His heart and need to care for people overruled his suspicions of the man, but not Brick's.

As far as he was concerned, Roman Furrow was still an unknown, and he would stay that way until Brick got some answers.

Chapter Six

Roman stared out the window at the lights coming from the top of the hill at the end of the peninsula. The room he was in felt homier than any of the fifty-odd rooms in his father's mansion. This room exuded family and comfort with its hand-stitched comforter, old, mismatched furniture, lace doilies, and floral wallpaper.

In his entire life, he'd never been as relaxed as he was right now in the home of someone who had no reason to care about his rest and had every reason to despise him and his family. He should have known something was up when Stephan said it was the Matthews's place he was buying. But much to his dismay, Roman was shown once again why his father wasn't to be trusted.

He'd wanted the sale to be on the up and up so he could finally see some improvement in his father's behavior. He knew better, but he still wanted to believe there was something salvageable between them. Today only further confirmed he was holding onto a dream, and the reality of things was clear.

Stephan Furrow was only concerned about himself. There was nothing left for his only son.

Roman heard a single set of footsteps pass by his room and then a second stepping into the room beside his. He wasn't sure if it was Fletch or Brick in the bedroom to his left, and he caught himself hoping it was Brick. The man fascinated Roman, and his body's reaction to Brick's touch was hard to ignore, but he had to. This wasn't the time or place for what he wanted to do with the handsome Navy SEAL.

Lightning flashed across the sky, lighting up his room as the thunder felt like it shook the earth. The storm was getting worse, and he couldn't imagine being out in it. He'd already sent an email off to his assistant and his mother, letting them know about the events of the day.

His mother wanted to send her new husband out to get him, but after a few moments of calming her down, she accepted he was fine and could make it back to Dallas on his own.

Overprotective described Janice Furrow to a T even if he was thirty-six. She loved him and made no attempt to hide it, much to her new husband's chagrin. Many a vacation had been cut short when his mother decided she'd been away from Roman for too long, and, apparently, her husband was none too pleased. Johnathan Waters had married Roman's mother over three years ago, and, according to her, they still behaved like newlyweds. His mother was happy, and it was all that mattered.

Roman's assistant had been working for him since he took over Furrow and Son, and he would be lost without him. Rick was what administration assistants dream to be, Roman's right hand. Loyal beyond reproach and smart as a whip. If he didn't know something, he'd move heaven and earth to find the answer. He was able to keep Roman on schedule and ready for every meeting.

Rick's response to the events of that day was his usual 'he's an asshole,' and 'your father needs a minder." He'd been correct, and Roman decided to hold interviews for a full-time handler of sorts. That would free up a lot of his time for business-related ventures, which would enhance the company's holdings.

It had concerned Roman when Brick and Fletch had pointed out the oddity of his accidents. Of course, he'd thought the same things they had, but without proof, there was nothing he could do except be on alert anytime he was out in public. What he didn't need was two retired Navy SEALs digging into something he was already aware of.

The detective back in Dallas had kept Roman's case open but doubted they'd find anything of use to uncover who these people were. Roman wasn't holding his breath.

His exhaustion overtook him, and his eyes fluttered closed. Roman welcomed it. Soon he was drifting away to the melody of rain and thunder, and he'd never felt more comfortable.

***

"Get up," someone yelled while grabbing onto Roman's arm.

He sprang up from the bed with his fists at the ready out of instinct, but he realized the "intruder" was Fletch. "What the hell?"

"Hell's about right. We're in the middle of it. Now get up. There's a tornado warning in the area, and we have to get down into the cellar."

Oh shit. The storm had morphed into something much worse. Roman slid on his shoes, grabbed his phone, and followed Fletch out of the room. The house was shaking in the wind as gusts forced open the garden doors allowing nature's fury into the house. He caught a glimpse of Brick out on the porch facing the lake like a warrior facing his foe. Lightning flashed highlighting the man's hard edges as he stared straight at the lake.

The rain lashed at Roman and Fletch as the wind pushed them back against the kitchen counter. Fletch's big hand took hold of his wrist, and he led Roman out the back door, down the steps, and up to a set of wooden doors attached to a concrete base leading underground.

"Get in," Fletch yelled, trying to be heard over the freight train bearing down on them, his muscles straining as he fought to hold the door open.

Roman didn't question him. He dove into the cellar and made his way to the back using his phone's flashlight. Fletch jumped in behind him and shut the doors.

"Wait. What about Brick? He's still out there." What happened to never leaving a man behind?

"He'll be fine."

"Fine? Have you lost your mind? He's out there in the open. We have to go get him." Roman pushed past Fletch and was about to open one of the doors when it flew wide on its own.

A lone figure stood out in the rain backlit by lightning crisscrossing the sky for another few seconds before racing in and shutting the doors behind him. Brick stood soaked to the bone, his clothing torn in places, a colorful cement turtle under his arm, and a sizeable gash on his head.

Fletch went to secure the doors when Brick asked, "Where the hell were you going?"

"To get you, you psycho. Standing out there like you're going to take on the storm all by yourself. You could've been killed."

Brick's head snapped back. "You were coming to save me?"

"I don't know what the hell I was going to do, but dragging you back here crossed my mind," Roman shouted as he reached for the first aid kit hanging on the wall. "Sit down and let me have a look at your head. Maybe it knocked some sense into you."

Without arguing any further, Brick set down the turtle and sat on a nearby chair, surprising Roman who'd been ready for an argument. He cleaned the wound, which wasn't as bad as the blood loss suggested, and after ten minutes of applying pressure, the cut stopped bleeding. The wind lashed at the cellar doors, but they remained locked tight. Roman reached into the kit and took out one of the instant cold packs, cracked whatever the hell was inside of those things, and shook it out as it began to chill.

"Here," Roman said while handing Brick the ice pack. "Hold that to your head while I wipe the blood off the side of your face."

Fletch was busy tuning a battery-operated radio while holding his phone for light, obviously checking for any news on the storm. Brick's dark eyes followed Roman's every move making the moment feel more intimate than it should've been. He wet a facecloth from the bag with the bottled water and leaned closer to wash the streaks of red from the side of Brick's head and neck.

The move brought him to within inches of the handsome SEAL in the confines of the root cellar. Roman could feel Brick's warm breath against his skin inviting him closer. A scent distinctly Brick's filled his senses, woodsy with a hint of leather and lake. It shouldn't work, but on Brick it did.

Although all the blood was cleaned away, Roman was having a hard time moving back. It felt as though he was trapped by Brick's gaze.

"I believe I got it all," he said, still not moving away.

"Thanks," Brick replied but remained in place, inches from Roman.

Just when he was about to dive into those luscious lips, the doors flew open, sending everything in the cellar swirling with the force of the powerful wind. Before he had a chance to react, Roman was pushed against the far wall as a big body covered him. Brick.

He could hear Fletch cursing while fighting with the doors as thunder roared all around them. Roman couldn't see what was happening from behind Brick's wide shoulders, and he had to admit, he probably didn't want to. His body was shaking uncontrollably.

Hell, he'd never faced a situation like this, but the calm demeanor coming off the former SEALS was a balm. They seemed like this was run of the mill for them.

Brick pressed closer. "It'll be okay, I've got you," he said in Roman's ear. "I won't let anything happen to you."

Damned if it didn't work. Roman's breathing slowed slightly, and his shaking was taken down a few notches. This was all screwed up. If he survived this, he'd be on his way in the morning. This man was essentially a stranger, so why did he trust Brick would protect him?

It hadn't even been twenty-four hours since he first met Brick. He had to be losing his mind after all that had happened in such a short period of time. Probably shock or something like it.

It was the only logical answer.

***

Brick could feel the wind and debris battering his back as Fletch struggled to shut the doors. Roman's hands curled against his chest shook as the world thundered around them. No civilian ever expects to be thrown into a life-threatening situation, but for Brick, chaos and life and death played out regularly over the course of his career. He'd been trained to within an inch of his life, preparing him to evaluate and think logically in extreme situations.

However, logic had flown out the root cellar at the feel of Roman's body up against his. Hell, he'd almost kissed the guy earlier when Roman was taking care of his head wound. It felt odd and exciting, confusing the shit out of him. Now wasn't the time to explore these conflicting desires no matter what his body wanted. He had to protect Roman, not bed him.

The slap of the wood doors closing signaled Fletch's success and ended to the need to cover Roman. Reluctantly, Brick stepped back allowing Roman to move freely. Brick went to help his friend secure the doors.

"We'll have to replace these doors and fortify the cellar before the next bad storm heads our way." Brick hammered an old two-by-four onto the door and overlapped them onto the concrete base surrounding it, giving them the leverage to stop the wind from sucking them open.

"It's on the priority list after we assess the damage to the house," Fletch stated.

"Yeah, don't remind me." With the sounds of glass breaking, his gut felt like it was being punched.

Sophia's lake house was taking a battering, and there was nothing he could do to stop it. All the work they'd already done could be ruined. Hell, the entire house could be leveled.

"It'll be okay," Roman offered from behind them. "The storm appears to be moving away from Fire Lake."

Brick turned to find Roman looking down at his cellphone. The screen was smashed, but it appeared to be still working under the spiderwebbed glass. Roman held it out for them to see the local radar, and sure enough, the worst had passed.

"Thank god. We might as well hunker down. There's no use going outside until we have some daylight. It's still too dangerous, and there's no need to leave." Brick knew it wasn't the time to check on the damage even though it was killing him not knowing.

"Yes, sir," Fletch agreed. He'd been getting better about not being formal about their ranks as often as he used to, but under the hostile circumstances, Brick understood why he fell back into their former roles.

The wind was still blowing, and rain was pouring down, but both were gradually slowing. Brick grabbed an old sleeping bag from the mess on the floor and handed it too Roman.

"You can bunk at the back of the cellar. Fletch and I will keep an eye on things, but I doubt it should pick up again."

"Thanks," Roman said as he took the sleeping bag and headed for where Brick had indicated. It was drier and not in direct line with the doors if they flew open again.

Brick cleared an area on the lower steps and sat down. His back ached, but he was sure the damage was nothing more than bruises. Fletch took a spot opposite him, still watching the radar to ensure no more surprises were in store.

It'd been a day from hell, but when he looked over at the handsome man in the faded red sleeping bag, Brick couldn't help but feel fortunate.

How messed up was that?

Chapter Seven

Roman looked out his office window at the Dallas skyline with its tall shiny buildings, most created by big oil. The Bank of America stood at seventy-two stories, Reunion Tower with its giant ball observation platform, and the pointed Fountain Place tower at sixty stories were among some of the most notable buildings in the city.

His offices took up three floors of one of the smaller buildings mixed into the metropolis that made this city hum. Floors forty up to and including forty-two belonged to Furrow and Son Investments, and his office was on the forty-second floor.

Dark and austere, he hadn't bothered to change it from his father's design esthetic. The man liked to present an all-powerful persona, and Roman chose to ignore it until the company was on better footing. He could work from anywhere, and he often found himself a spot in the company library or even the filing room. Rick always knew where to find him.

His assistant buzzed between all three floors daily with the energy of a meerkat who'd eaten a bag of sugar. There was zero chance of Roman disappearing even if he wanted to at times. He'd received the new quarterly report, and the company was still on track to outpace last year's growth, which should have him dancing on his desk, but he was unsettled.

It'd been over a week since that terrifying night spent in the cellar. The F2 tornado had ripped a dotted path from Kerrville to Vanderpool before being downgraded to a severe thunderstorm. Thankfully, Sophia's house was miles away from the epicenter and survived with only minor damage. However, sadly a trailer park directly in the path of the tornado did not.

When they'd emerged from the root cellar the following morning, the area was covered in debris. Trees had been uprooted, large branches lay covering the yard, and what looked to be a new shed had been leveled, which seemed to bother Brick the most. A few windows had been smashed out by flying debris, and the fishing boat broke away from the dock and lay overturned in the long grass over fifty yards away, mooring hooks still attached.

The roof had held, which saved the interior from most of the damage. Of course, the broken windows and open garden doors had allowed the wind and rain to get into a few areas, but most of the house remained dry. All and all, the house was in much better shape than expected, and he'd seen the relief on Brick's face when they resurfaced.

As promised, a tow truck came out that morning, which surprised Roman a bit considering the severity of the storm, and towed him to Marshall. He'd arrived back in Dallas later that day but still couldn't put the experience behind him.

It could've been the shock of going through something so traumatic. Or perhaps it was the knock down drag 'em out fight he'd had with Stephan when they returned to his father's home. Although he knew his father was an asshole, he didn't expect his father to disown him. Which, technically, didn't matter as it applied to the company, but it'd hurt, thought it didn't change their fucked-up relationship.

Then again, it could've been the handsome Navy SEAL who protected Roman with his body.

He had been going with shock. And yes, he knew he was in denial.

"If that isn't a look of longing, I don't know what is. What happened? You get ghosted by your latest conquest?" Rick asked as he bounded in with more energy than was warranted. He placed more files on Roman's desk and insisted, "Spill it. Someone new?" Yes, Rick was his assistant, but he was also Roman's friend.

"No. No one new," Roman said while reaching for the files.

Rick's perfectly plucked eyebrows flew up. "The big bad Navy guy." When Roman didn't answer, he continued. "Well, well, you like them tattooed and muscled, I see. That's new."

"What do you mean?"

"Your MO has always seemed to run toward the business professional types. You know, suits, after work drinks, and a quick roll between the sheets."

"Since when do I have an MO?" He'd never realized he had a type.

"Need I remind you of Pablo, the account executive from Fort Worth, Sean the investment banker from Austin, Samuel the head of research and development from Waco, he shuttered, and Daniel from that startup that'd made the list of the top twenty up and coming businesses in Dallas."

"Daniel," Roman laughed. "I almost forgot about him. I wonder how his company is doing now?" They'd only dated a couple of times.

"The way of the Dodo," Rick answered while shaking his head. "At least for him."

"But the company was worth over nine million dollars in only two short years. What the hell happened?" Roman asked as he sat back behind his desk and took out a pen. "Daniel had been positive he'd double that in the next year."

"Officially, Daniel was bought out of his shares by his partners."

"Unofficially?"

"Daniel's got himself a new habit." Rick tapped the side of his nose. "Cocaine."

"I wondered about that. When we'd go out, he never seemed exhausted. A new tech startup, working extremely long hours and still able to go out until the wee hours of the morning. No one can keep up that schedule without passing out on their feet."

"I watched a documentary about cocaine use in Silicon Valley a couple of weeks ago. It was quite the lesson, let me tell you. Anyway, they use it to stay awake and be more productive, leading to heroin and prescription drug use. Word on the street is, Daniel was caught doing lines at a party and overdosed. Since the buyout, Daniel's been pretty much off the radar."

"Hopefully, he's found help with his addiction. He was a normal guy in a difficult industry where the competition is fierce," Roman couldn't help but feel sorry for him. "Maybe that's why he called me?"

"Daniel called you?" Rick gasped. "And you didn't tell me? When?"

"Six or eight months ago he left a message, but when I called him back, it went to voicemail, which was full. I never heard back from him." Roman had assumed it wasn't urgent when Daniel never called again. Maybe he should've tried harder to reach him.

"How did you two meet again?"

"I was at a charity fundraiser, and he came over and introduced himself," Roman remembered it because he'd barely gotten in the door when Daniel came over to him.

"Sign here," Rick said as he pointed to a line on the sheet in front of him. "And there. I've removed clause six as you asked."

"Thanks. How they thought I'd allow that kind of concession is mind-boggling." Roman shouldn't have been so shocked.

"Probably thought you'd miss it or accept it as your father had."

"Firing employees without cause will never happen while I lead this company. People need security to work at their best."

One particular wing of Furrow and Son had been a pain in Roman's ass since he took over years ago. Stephan had allowed the team to make their own rules for so many years that reigning them in was proving to be more of a chess match. There were five members, and their office was on the fortieth floor. Their team dealt with resource allocations and was headed by a personal friend of Stephan's, Maxwell.

The only reason Roman hadn't fired all five of them was because of their spotless track record. Instead, he sent three tried and tested employees from other positions in the company who wouldn't run at the first sign of trouble to join the team. Hence their latest request.

"When will they accept Stephan isn't coming back and these changes are not going away?"

"At least their weekly list of complaints/demands is under two pages this time."

"Like we don't have enough to deal with. Do me a favor, see if you can dig anything up on Daniel." He had to make sure the guy was okay and couldn't help but wonder if the phone call was a cry for help he'd missed.

Rick gave him a concerned look. "You're not looking to rekindle anything, right?"

"No. I want to make sure he'd all right. In treatment, and not out on the street. Nothing romantic, but I can't not help if he needs it."

"You're too soft, boss. I've told you before you can't save everyone." Rick's heart was in the right place trying to protect Roman, but he couldn't be like his father and only watch out for himself.

"Yeah, yeah, yeah. What else you got for me?"

"That's all for now," Rick said before taking a seat in a nearby chair. "So, this Navy SEAL hot?"

Roman should've known he wouldn't get out of this conversation so easily. "If you must know, yes, he's handsome, in a kick-your-ass kinda way."

"Nice, and…."

"And what?"

"Come on, all I got was a dark-haired veteran with tattoos. I want details, and does he have a friend for me?"

Roman couldn't help but laugh. Rick never behaved this way if others were around. He was the consummate professional. "He has a friend named Fletcher, and I believe they served together at some point because he occasionally referred to Brick as 'sir.' As for details, I wasn't there that long, but he has several tattoos across his arms, chest, and stomach."

Rick raised an eyebrow, and gave Roman an insistent glare.

"Fine. He has '*La Vida Loca*' under his collar bone and a large 1983 across his chest. On the left side of his abdomen written in cursive is the word 'Trust,' and his left arm had a smashed clock and what looked like a village. His right arm was much the same, so I'm guessing each has some sort of special meaning."

"Trust makes sense, and so does *La Vida Loca*. The crazy life considering his career choice. Hell, for all we know, he could have been born in 1983, as his chest suggests." Rick loved a mystery. "Anything else other than his glorious muscles."

"His right nipple is pierced."

"Holy shit. How did you manage to keep your hands to yourself?" Rick was not shy and Roman often wondered why the guy wasn't permanently hooked up. He always went after what he wanted.

"That was easy. The guy hates me." Along with a host of other people, which sucked.

"The guy hates your father," Rick corrected as he sat in one of the chairs in front of Roman's desk.

"Trust me when I tell you, many people paint me with the same brush as Stephan." Even though they were worlds apart.

"You're nothing like him. If Mr. *Vida Loca* couldn't see that then good riddance."

"Leave it at I don't expect to receive an invite back to the lake house."

"Just when I think your old man couldn't get any lower, he tries to force a young woman into prostituting herself so he could get that property. I honestly think he's losing it."

"You and me both," a woman's voice declared from the doorway.

Rick bolted out of his seat and stood straight as a pin as Janice Furrow Waters strolled in with an outlandish feathered hat and designer handbag to match.

"Hello, mother," Roman said as he came out from behind his desk to meet her halfway with a hug. "You look wonderful as always. What brings you by?"

She hugged him tight, and he could feel her love in every touch, or he liked to assume that was the way it was. His mother had a hard time conceiving, and when Roman came along, he was considered a miracle. Well, at least by one parent.

When she finally released him, Janice looked over at Rick and said, "Cut it out with prim, proper assistant routine. I know better."

Rick eased his stance and let out a long breath. "Yes, ma'am. I'll leave you two alone."

"Thank you," she said before turning her attention back to Roman. "You look tired. What's wrong?"

"Nothing's wrong. The quarterlies came in, and we're right on target."

"Are you working too much?" she asked, not buying his change in subject.

"When am I not working too much?" He couldn't help but tease as he led his mother over to one of the two couches. "Don't worry so much. We both know what it's going to take to turn this company around, and I'm willing to do it."

"Your grandfather would be proud of the man you've become. He knew what he was doing when he left his portion of the company to you. I worry though that's all you have is this company. You shouldn't be so alone in everything."

Red alert. His mother was working up to something.

"You should have someone of your own to come home to. To help carry your load and comfort you when you need it." She took hold of his hand.

Defcon one. Here it comes.

"I met this nice young man at the club. He's the son of the LeClair's, from LeClair Oil. His name is Thomas, and he's single. I could arrange a nice dinner at the club for the two of you to meet and get to know each other. You never know what might happen."

Roman took a few heartbeats before responding. "Um, mom, you know I love you."

"Of course, I do, and I love you even more. That's why I found this nice man for you to meet. I worry. You're all alone, and you're not getting any younger. It scares me to think when I'm gone, there'll be no one to look after you."

Roman's father wasn't the only one who knew how to use emotional blackmail, but at least his mother used her power for good, or at least what she thought was good.

He let out a deep breath and gave the only acceptable answer. "Sounds great, mom."

Lord help him.

Chapter Eight

Brick hammered the final nail into place on the side of the shed for the second time in as many months. He and Fletch had made a substantial dent in the repairs needed to the property from the storm damage. They'd buttoned up the house the first day after the storm and headed off to Kerrville to help with the search and rescue operations taking place along the tornado's path. The mangled mass of buildings reminded him of other war-torn areas across the globe. Mother nature could be a real bitch when she wanted to.

They'd gotten back two days ago and had been working on cleanup ever since. Considering this was the second crack at rebuilding this shed, he'd used extra reinforcements this time around. Brick would be damned if he rebuilt it for a third time.

The new boat was back at the marina having repairs done while the old aluminum fishing boat was still up a tree. The new windows arrived yesterday, fallen trees had been cut up for firewood, and the new steel doors had been installed on the newly reinforced storm cellar.

With all the shit going on around him, you'd think Brick wouldn't have to fight to remain focused. Roman Furrow was to blame, and never far away from his thoughts. Brick was still waiting on that report from Spence on the guy's run of bad luck. However, it was more than that. Every time he turned around, his mind wandered back to those panicked blue eyes.

Despite how afraid Roman had been, he'd tried to push his way out of the safety of the cellar to get to Brick. That one act spoke volumes about the type of man Roman was. Far more than simply words ever could. In high-pressure situations, your true self comes out, and Roman was no different, but instead of concentrating on his own welfare, he was concerned about Brick.

He threw his tools back into the box and stood, stretching out his back as he did. Fletch was busy replacing a few of the shingles that had gotten torn off by the one-hundred miles per hour wind. They'd been fortunate this time around but would plan better in case their luck didn't hold.

Dusting the dirt off his pants, Brick walked up to the porch and went inside in search of something cold to drink. An eighties rock song filled the living room and kitchen as Julia liked to have the radio on while she worked. She and her son, Sammy, had been safely tucked in the basement of their home when the storm hit. Thankfully, neither was hurt.

It became clear that Julia had been a godsend since she started working for him. She was highly organized and driven, and Brick had no doubt she'd have them on track in no time.

"How's it going?" he asked as he walked by the dining table to get to the fridge.

"Good," she said. "I've made my way through the books on the shelf and found a few things that I thought might interest you."

Brick took a long drink from his glass of water before joining her at the table. "What did you find?"

"A few old letters and photos stuck in between the pages so far. I left them on the same pages as I found them in case it was important."

He looked down at a small pile of maybe five books and picked up one. Inside was a picture of him when he was young and his rainbow turtle. Brick couldn't help but smile at the memory he hadn't shared with anyone else. It remained between Sophia and him alone.

The second book had two letters flattened between separate pages. The first one he opened seemed to be well-read by the multiple different folds crossing the page. It was from someone named Gerald, no last name. On the stained page with edges darkened by time was a single sentence. "Love is composed of a single soul inhabiting two bodies." Underneath was a handwritten diagram of a forest with directions.

"What the hell?"

"It's Aristotle. I think it's meant to be a love note," Julia said. "Your great-aunt had a gentleman caller."

"Hmm, I don't remember ever seeing Sophia with a man. Then again, I wasn't here all the time, so, it was possible."

"It's nice to think she wasn't always alone," Julia hummed.

As the young woman fantasized about fairytales or some shit, Brick's phone began ringing. "Excuse me," he said as he stepped away and answered the call.

"Brick here."

"Hey, buddy." Spence's scratchy voice came on the line. "Got some information for you. Are you far from your laptop?"

"Hold on," Brick said as he grabbed his computer and brought it over to the coffee table before sitting. Once it came to life, he said, "Ready."

Files began popping up on his screen. He wasn't sure how Spence did what he did. Brick was simply happy he was on the side of good. Mostly.

"Any breakdown you want to give me before I trudge through all these files?" Damn, he hoped so because that was a lot of reading.

"Yeah, your new friend has pissed off somebody because the word isn't good. He's being targeted. I don't know if it's actually to kill him or simply rough him up," Spence stated plainly without emotion.

"Shit. Who's the head of this snake?" Knowing who was behind it would help him decide how to deal with it.

"I'm still working on that bit of information. I'll get it to you the moment I know more. I also investigated Roman's company, and while most are happy about the leadership change, there are a few lamenting about the good old days, which confuses me because the good old days weren't that good. The company was a dumpster fire ready to implode before the son took over."

Brick opened the first file, which turned out to be a listing of ER visits Roman had made in the last two years. It was lengthy. "Shit, I'm surprised he's not in traction by now."

"No kidding, dude."

"Thanks, Spence."

"We'll talk soon."

He barely registered putting the phone down on the coffee table, too engrossed in reading the misadventures in the last two years in the life of Roman Furrow. It wasn't pretty, and the incidents seemed to be accelerating in the level of violence, making Brick wonder if they were working their nerve up to do the final deed and kill the new head of Furrow and Son Investments.

Brick was involved now, and he wasn't going let anything happen to Roman on his watch.

***

It'd been a long day and all Roman wanted to do was go home, pour himself a beer and relax before having to do it all over again tomorrow. A day of endless meetings always had this effect on him, but it couldn't be avoided. The company was turning around, and the Furrow name no longer elicited a cringe from others in the business community. He needed to ride the wave of change he was creating.

He waved good night to the security guard manning the lobby and struck out into the warm summer night with its streetlights and glowing buildings. Roman liked this time of day. It was as close to peaceful as downtown Dallas got. He walked across to the opposite side of the street to the parking garage. Only three cars were still parked on the street.

When he pushed the button for the elevator, he felt pinpricks running down his back, giving him the feeling of being watched. Roman turned around and scanned the parking garage but found nothing unusual. His nerves had him on edge and more jumpy than typical, but nothing had happened to him in days, so he saw danger all around him.

"Cut this shit out," Roman whispered to himself. "You're fine."

The sharp ding of the elevator made him jump as the doors opened to reveal nothing inside. Letting out a deep breath, he stepped on board and the doors shut behind him. He'd parked on the third floor today. No special parking for him. He could walk.

His date the other night with Thomas LeClair went as expected. Soul-crushing, He hoped he wasn't that boring and pretentious when he talked about work. Thomas name-dropped the 75205 ZIP code, one of the upper-tier communities in Dallas, like it was his private Rolodex. Serious turn-off. After a cursory goodnight kiss Roman went home alone.

The elevator dinged as it reached the third floor, and when the doors opened, he stepped off into a typical parking garage. Grey concrete, dark, and everything smelled like oil and exhaust. There had to be a way to make these places less frightening.

Several vehicles were parked on his level, attesting to many late nights in the office buildings surrounding the area. Roman's car wasn't too far away, so he hit the unlock button on his key fob, making the car's horn beep. He took a few more steps up the ramp when his car beeped again and locked.

Roman stopped and looked down at his key fob, hit the unlock again, and took a few more steps before the same thing happened.

"What the hell?" Was his remote broken?

About twenty yards away, headlights flashed on, blinding him for a second. He hadn't seen anybody else in the parking garage, but they could've walked up the stairs instead of using the elevator. He had to remain logical. Letting his imagination run wild wouldn't help.

He unlocked his car doors again, but when it beeped, the other car squealed forward, heading straight for him. Roman wasn't an idiot and began running in the other direction and around a concrete post that had to be three feet thick. The car sideswiped the post before turning the corner and stopping on the ramp down to the second level.

The white of the taillights had him running once again to his car and safety. When he was within a few feet, the car beeped and locked once again. Roman desperately tried to unlock the doors, but his fingers fumbled with the key fob. He could hear the other car getting closer as he fought with the doors.

This was it. Whoever had been following him had Roman exactly where they wanted him. He closed his eyes, not wanting to see the hit coming, when he heard another vehicle coming squealing from the other direction from the fourth floor.

He opened his eyes as the second car came to a screeching halt beside him, protecting him from the original car. Roman wasn't sure he could believe his eyes, but Brick jumped out of the driver's seat and Fletcher from the passengers, both pointing guns at the car that had chased Roman through the parking garage.

The mystery car immediately slammed on its breaks and punched it into reverse, leaving without a bullet being fired. The world around Roman seemed surreal as he fought to stop his hands from shaking. He felt like his body was going to splinter apart. He wondered if he was having a panic attack.

"Roman," Brick spoke softly, his gruff voice rumbling low. "It's okay," he said as he slowly wrapped an arm around Roman and held him close. "Told you I wouldn't let anything happen to you."

"Brick, how...." Roman's voice shook as he spoke.

"Not important right now. I'll explain everything once we're back at the lake house," Brick assured him.

"We're going to Sophia's?" Roman couldn't hide his surprise. He never thought he'd be invited there again.

"It'll be easier to protect you there. Unless you want to stay here and try your luck," Brick said. Roman didn't miss he'd used the same line as the night of the storm. In other words, *I can protect you better than you can take care yourself.* True, but demoralizing.

"I can work remotely." He wasn't stupid. He wasn't sticking around to wait for whoever was targeting him to come back and have another go.

"Good choice." Brick smiled causing Roman lean into his body.

"Cops are on their way," Fletch announced as he joined them. "I couldn't get a good look at the driver. The windows were tinted."

"Neither could I," Brick said. "Roman. Let's get you sitting before you pass out, man."

He was in no condition to argue, so he followed Brick to the back of his car and took a seat. Roman raked his hand through his hair as he tried to piece together what happened and why. It seemed likely whoever was driving that car would've run him over if these guys hadn't come along.

"Brick." Roman watched as serious dark eyes zeroed in on him. "Is someone trying to kill me?"

The big Navy SEAL took a moment before answering, making him wonder if he was trying to soften the blow.

"Yes."

"Where was the sugarcoating?" Roman's voice had never been so high.

"I won't do that to you. I respect you enough to be honest."

"I guess that's better than hate."

"The jury is still out on you. I don't hate you yet."

"Gee, thanks," Roman laughed at the absurdity of the situation. Someone had tried to kill him, and here he was trading jabs with Brick like they were sitting around shooting shit.

Chapter Nine

Brick kept his eyes on the back window as Fletch drove their rental car back from Dallas. Roman had fallen asleep in the back seat almost immediately, and Brick could understand the adrenaline crash on top of some seriously long hours the man put in. They'd been watching him for the past few days and had Roman's routine down.

The guy was up before dawn and at the office hours before anyone else even got out of bed. Most nights, he stayed later than anyone else. The only time he'd seen Roman take a break was for dinner with some over-inflated suit. Brick didn't like it. The only saving grace was that Roman didn't seem to have a good time either.

They'd decided on a rental because Brick's vehicle was identifiable and would lead them back to the lake house. Of course, they didn't rent one from Marshall as that was too close to home. They decided to move a couple of counties east before parking his truck and securing a rental car.

"See anything?" Fletch asked, never once taking his eyes off the road.

"No, we're clear. No one's following us."

"That was close," Fletch said in his normally booming voice, not worrying about waking Roman up.

"Shh, he's sleeping."

Fletch raised one bushy eyebrow and whispered, "Sorry."

"Yeah, it was too damn close. If we hadn't been waiting for him to come out of his building, Roman would have been killed in a hit and run. Like his other accidents, without witnesses or leads."

"Yeah, that Detective didn't have shit," Fletch huffed. "What's he been doing all this time?"

"Beats the shit out of me. I doubt he'll be of any use to us." Brick had to wonder about the guy.

"Yeah, I got that loud and clear," Fletch huffed.

"We should be back home by seven this morning. I'll give Spence a call. We need more information on Detective Moses." The guy gave Brick a bad feeling, and early on, he'd learned to listen to his gut.

"Agreed. What do we do in the meantime?"

"Protect Roman until we figure out who's after him."

"Then what?" Fletch asked.

"We return to our previously scheduled programming," Brick said as non-committal as possible.

Fletch glanced over at him with a doubtful expression. "Right."

***

The first couple of days working remotely had been a lesson in patience, considering all the moving parts. Meetings were held virtually in his room/office in front of a white sheet hanging from thumbtacks. He'd gotten a crash course on all the ways his communications could be tracked, and all the precautions he'd have to take to work remotely. Brick and Fletch had destroyed his cell phone in the Dallas parking garage and threw it in a trash bin. Rick kept him up to date and on track via copious and detailed emails, none of which Roman answered directly. All return communications to Rick were sent to cloud storage, which he then downloaded. Spence rerouted Roman's Skype and Zoom meetings so if back-traced, it looked like he was in Alaska. If whoever was trying to hurt him wanted to see the company fall apart, they'd sooner see hell freeze over than Furrow and Son Investments go down.

The press had gotten a hold of the story and were running with the headline, "Furrow's CEO and savior a marked man." Seriously, he didn't need any bad press or signs of weakness, not now when trying to present and maintain a stable image of the company.

Rick had taken the news of the threat reasonably well. Early on, he'd become suspicious of all the minor "accidents," and had given Roman a can of mace. As the "accidents" escalated, Rick gave him a set of brass knuckles. His mother, on the other hand, went full out Momma bear, insisting on hiring a team of bodyguards to protect him as well as demanding to know where he was.

Roman felt bad about not telling her his location, but Brick had made it clear: no one was to know. It made sense. It wasn't as if they wanted any surprise visitors. Yes, his father's home was on the same peninsula, but Stephan Furrow had left for Italy the night after the tornado struck and had no plans of returning anytime soon. There was no chance of him driving by and seeing Roman on the lake house property even if his father was home. The house was set back from the road, and Roman wasn't hanging around outside where people could see him.

Julia had offered to help get him organized, and Roman was thankful for her help. She'd ordered a new laptop for him—more precautions—and she'd ordered office equipment: a desk, chair, a printer/scanner, and they had killer internet installed.

For the most part, it worked, and he was thankful for all the help, and for being kept safe and protected. He tried to help out around the house when he wasn't in meetings or reading through pages of reports, analytics, and predictions. He had to remain vigilant about all the markets to make sure their investors felt as secure as possible.

Roman had been on the phone all morning and decided to take his laptop out onto the porch to get some fresh air. The only time he wore a suit jacket, button down shirt and tie was when he had video meetings. Usually, he was in his jeans and t-shirts, preferring them to his expertly tailored suits he used as the typical, expected conservative corporate armor.

He emerged from his room, laptop in hand, and headed out the new garden doors. A set of new patio furniture arrived yesterday, with a tiltable umbrella, which, at Brick's direction, he used to shield himself from prying eyes.

Roman took a spot on one of the well-cushioned chairs and set his laptop on the small table between him and another chair to his side. With a grin, he remembered the first day he came to sit out on the porch and nearly fell through a chair. These were certainly an improvement.

Fletch was out on the dock busy installing more mooring cleats to the opposite side of the originals. He wondered if they were getting another boat and decided he wouldn't ask since it wasn't his business. He was here to be protected until the person or people behind all the attempts on his life was caught. He was still perplexed as to why Brick and Fletch decided to protect him of all people, but he was beyond grateful. If they hadn't shown up, he'd likely be dead. A chill ran through his body at the thought.

"It's here," Julia called out as she joined him on the porch carrying a box. When he went to help, she shooed him off. "I've got it."

She set it down on a nearby table and began ripping into the packaging. Roman could make out the image on the side of the box once the wrapping was gone.

"A coffee maker?"

With a quick intake of breath, Julia acted like he's insulted her somehow. "Not merely a coffee maker. *The* coffee maker sent by angels in heaven. It brews drip coffee, cappuccinos, espresso, cold brews, specialty coffees." She stopped to hug the box. "Real coffee."

"Is that why you asked me what type of coffee I liked?" Days ago, she'd come to his room, which he left open if he wasn't on a call, and asked him to name his favorite brews.

"Yeah, Brick wanted me to make sure there was something you liked stocked."

"He did?" Roman asked, surprised something so mundane and domestic would cross Brick's mind.

Julia looked at him like he'd grown a second head. "Did you notice the patio furniture suddenly appear?"

"Yes, of course, I noticed." It made a significant difference to the porch.

"Right after you fell through one of the old chairs."

"Sounds about right. You don't want dangerous furniture around."

Julia stood staring at him even harder if that were possible. "Men. How were you guys ever considered the smarter sex?"

Before Roman could ask what she meant by that, Brick came around the front corner of the house. Seeing them on the porch, he changed directions and headed straight for them.

"I see your new baby came," Brick said to Julia, who beamed with happiness.

"Yes, and I can't wait to set it up." She bounced in excitement. "I'm going to read over the manual. Be ready for after supper coffee tonight."

"I have no doubt," Brick said as he sat down in a chair near Roman's.

Julia hugged the box again and took it inside to no doubt set it up. Brick looked tired and hot. It was in the high eighties in the shade.

"I'll get you something to drink," Roman offered before heading for the door.

"Make it a beer, and feel free to join me with one of your own."

Roman couldn't help but smile at his generosity. He'd tried to give Brick money to help pay for his food and upkeep while he stayed there, but the Navy SEAL refused outright. "You're our guest here," was all he'd said as if that explained everything. Roman knew he wasn't a guest. He was being safeguarded by two of the deadliest men the US military trained.

When he returned with the beers, Brick seemed satisfied that Roman had gotten one as well. He handed Brick's to him, and for a second, their fingers touched, and that same damn zing of awareness he associated with Brick happened again.

As calmly as possible, he sat in his chair and tried to get himself under control. Roman spied the rainbow turtle Brick had risked his life to save during the storm sitting in the corner of the deck. Safe and sound.

"That's the turtle from the other night in the cellar," Roman said.

Brick looked over and said, "Yep, that's the one."

When he didn't continue with more information, Roman couldn't fight the need to ask. "Why is it so important to you?"

Brick looked at him oddly, and Roman was close to apologizing when the big guy started talking.

"Sophia bought it for me when I was going through a rough patch at fifteen. My parents were divorcing, and I was struggling with my identity."

"That you're gay."

"Yeah, she knew, but she never came out and said it. That wasn't her way. Instead, one day, Sophia came back from grocery shopping with something that wasn't on the list."

Roman looked over at the turtle. "Him?"

"Yeah, the turtle, and single quart paint cans in a rainbow of colors. She said it was an art project for the two of us to do the next day because it was supposed to rain. I didn't think anything of it. As you've discovered, she had a lot of garden gnomes and other stuff, so the request didn't strike me as odd."

"I like Sophia more and more." Roman had noticed the concrete figures here and there. "She sounds amazing."

"She was," Brick confirmed. "There'll never be another like her." He shook his head. "Anyway, the next day, sure enough, it rained, and she set up our art project on the kitchen table, which was covered with newspapers. There was red, orange, yellow, green, blue, and violet paint poured out into cups."

"I guess your fifteen-year-old mind didn't put two and two together?"

"Hell no. Sophia handed me a brush and told me that she wanted the turtle painted in a neat rainbow, no paint splotches here or there, so that's what I did. I can still remember the rain pouring down outside as I painted her new turtle. We talked about my mom and dad and what divorce meant for me. She tried to convince me my parents still loved me no matter what, and I remember praying she was right. When I finished the turtle, she let it sit while we drank hot cocoa. When we went back to the table, she lifted the turtle to inspect it."

Roman was sucked into the story and could barely contain himself when Brick stopped talking. "Don't leave me hanging, man."

The one corner of Brick's lips pulled up into a half-smile. "Sophia said that she loved everything about rainbows and their uniqueness and the strength of each color. None of the colors matched the others, but each respected the other for their differences making each standout. She'd say something like the world was full of unique rainbows, and no one of them was better than the other. She held up the turtle, looked at me, and said, *This is your rainbow. You are special in every way, no matter what others think. Every time I look at this turtle, I'll know that my rainbow is out in the world making me proud no matter who you love.'"

"Wow. What an extraordinary lady," Roman said out of respect for the woman who took the time to guide a teenager through what was probably the most difficult and traumatic part of his life.

The moment was quiet, with only the odd duck breaking the silence. It felt serene and as the sun peaked around a cloud and shone on the surface of the water, otherworldly. This would've made an amazing photo.

Brick was silent as the two of them drank their beers and looked out onto the water. It was perfect, and it made him almost forget he didn't belong here, and someone was trying to kill him.

"Have you learned anything about who might be targeting me?"

Brick took another drink of his beer before saying, "It's narrowed down to a few individuals but first answer a question for me. Do you have a spare key for your car?"

"Yes. In a drawer somewhere at home. Why?"

"And where do you keep your key during the day?"

"In my pocket. I carry two keys on me at all times for the car and my apartment."

"What? You don't have a house on a hill like your father?" Fletch butted in as he joined them on the porch.

"No. I have an apartment in a building not far from my office. I don't need more."

Fletch's eyebrow went up. "Penthouse?"

"Nope."

Roman could understand their confusion. His father made a big first impression, and most of the time it was obnoxious and larger than life.

"Back to suspects." Brick cut in. "Your parents, stepfather, and Rick. Anyone who had access to your home. I was hoping you could tell us who else has access to your apartment."

"My parents? Why the hell would they want to hurt me?" Was Brick out of his mind? "I'm sure they both are capable of many things, but attempted murder?"

"Someone was messing with your car locks, correct?"

"Yeah, I'd unlock my car, and then it would relock. There could've been something wrong with my fob."

"Your car and remote have been cleared of any mechanical failure."

"How do you know this?"

"Detective Moses called to let Fletch know," Brick said. "No one can trace Fletch's burner phone, which means no one can trace him to Fire Lake, He's the designated go between."

"Why didn't he call me?"

"Because I told him you had enough to do keeping your company going from a distance. Would you rather he tried to call you?"

Roman thought about it for a moment. Did he want to know all the things going on behind the scenes while running Furrow's? Not a chance. He barely had time to eat as it was.

"I concede your point. Thank you."

Brick nodded. "Considering everything was in working order, that makes the possibility of someone grabbing your spare key and fob more likely."

It made sense even though he didn't want to think someone he had in his home wanted him dead. "Well, that sucks."

"Yeah, it blows when you can't trust family," Fletch agreed. "You're better off making your own family in this messed up world."

"Make your own family?"

"Yeah, like Brick and me. We're brothers from different mothers."

That made Roman smile, but he'd never had that opportunity. Most people saw him as his father's progeny or were hovering close because of his money. Other than Rick, he'd never gotten close to anyone else including the men he'd dated.

"That sounds nice," Roman said, unable to keep the yearning out of his voice. "I'll make you a list, but I want it known right from the start. Rick isn't involved."

"You two close," Brick asked without looking at him.

"He's been my brother from a different mother, as you say, and assistant for many years. I trust him completely."

"I'll take that under advisement," Brick stood, set his empty on the table, and looked down at him with those eyes Roman saw in his sleep. Dark, piercing, completely zoned in on him and him alone. "I'd like that list sooner than later."

"You'll have it within the hour."

"Good," he replied. "Fletch, get off your ass. We still have to deal with the brush around the new satellite dish."

"No rest for the wicked," Fletch grumbled and followed along. "How come I didn't get a beer break?"

Roman was left with his troubled thoughts. His father certainly had the vindictive nature to make it possible he was behind plotting to kill Roman. Shit, maybe disowning him wasn't all the old man had up his sleeve.

He ripped a piece of paper out of his new planner and began his list of possible assassins.

One thing he never in his life thought he'd have to do.

Chapter Ten

Brick rolled over on his bed and punched his pillow a couple more times, attempting to make it softer so he could fall asleep. It was two in the damn morning, and he still hadn't slept for even a moment. This was bullshit. He flipped over onto his back and stared at the ceiling, counting the stains from the previous leaky roof. He'd have to get around to ordering new drywall eventually, but there were bigger things to worry about.

He'd called in a few old friends to help with protecting Roman. They'd sounded eager to help and were already on their way. He and Fletch had set sensors up around the property in case they had any unannounced visitors, as well as a few rudimentary traps any deep-cover ops team would be proud of.

They had two handguns and a rifle on the property and wouldn't hesitate to use them if necessary. Now it was a matter of figuring out who was after Furrow and Son's new CEO. Roman's list wasn't long, which surprised Brick. Didn't CEO's throw parties and shit? He had to admit Roman wasn't adhering to the image he'd had of the man.

Roman wasn't like his father. He was anything but ruthless and untrustworthy. Instead, he exuded courage, passion, resilience, and drive. How had the son fallen so far from the tree?

What shocked him the most was he'd shared his private memory with Roman. Brick had never told anyone how his rainbow turtle came to be, not even his teammates. However, the words seemed to flow from his mouth when Roman asked. The most pain-filled moment in his life when his family was being torn apart, and his body was sending him mixed messages. He let it out without a second thought.

Brick could hear the clicking of a keyboard coming from Roman's room beside his own. What was he doing up so late? He'd noticed that Roman worked his butt off all day, barely taking a moment for himself, and now he was still working into the wee hours.

The more Brick thought, the more worked up he got. Stephan Furrow was off on a trip to Italy, living the good life off his son's hard work, and he doubted the father was the only one. By the speed of the clicks, the man's hands had to be flying across the keyboard. Almost a frantic pace.

When was Roman going to sleep? He got up early like the rest of them. More clicking. It was driving Brick nuts. He sat up in his bed and let out a deep huff before swinging his legs over the side of his bed and stood. Someone had to put a stop to this.

Dressed only in his boxer briefs, Brick left his room and walked the couple of feet over to Roman's door. He knocked softly and waited.

"Yes," Roman whispered.

Instead of answering, Brick opened the door to find Roman sitting behind his desk wearing only a towel around his waist. His mind went blank when confronted with the perfect male specimen. Of course, he'd seen Roman in his boxer's before when he was in the bathroom drying up from the storm, but he'd been more concerned with his wounds and scars to appreciate the package.

His shoulders were broad, and his arms were well defined along with his chest, which was covered in a light dusting of blond hair that led down to a treasure trail Brick wanted to explore.

"You should be sleeping," he said in a much gruffer voice than he had intended as he tried to get himself under control.

"Um, is my typing bothering you?" Roman asked, looking as confused as Brick was. "I'm sorry. I can move to the other side of the house."

"No, that's not it." Why were words suddenly difficult to speak? Damn, now he was getting a hardon, which normally happens when he desired someone. However, this wasn't the time or the man.

"What is it?"

Brick raked his palm down his face and said, "You need rest."

Roman's expression changed to an almost smile. "I will. Thank you for worrying about me."

"I wasn't worried about you," Brick shot out.

"Okay." Roman's head snapped back like he'd punched him.

Shit, he was screwing this up royally. "Go to sleep," Brick ordered, falling into Lieutenant Commander mode.

"Can I finish this last memo?" Roman asked.

"Yes, but then sleep."

"Yes, sir."

"Good," Brick stated then quickly shut the door as his cock stood at attention. Being called sir never garnered this kind of reaction before.

He went back into his room and closed the door quietly. Brick looked down at the tent in his boxer briefs, let out a huff, and stared at the ceiling again knowing he'd made things worse for himself.

Brilliant.

***

Roman looked back at the screen, unsure what just happened and desperately trying to push his hard shaft down so that Brick couldn't see it. What kind of impression would they have of him if he started lusting after the owner of a place his father tried to turn into a helipad?

He couldn't screw this up no matter what his cock wanted, and right now, he wanted Brick. Okay, he could admit there was a sexual attraction. He hadn't gotten laid in what felt like forever, so it made sense his body would react to Brick's cut abs, muscled thighs and... Cataloging Brick's physical attributes wasn't helping.

Turning his thoughts to Brick's willingness to put himself out there to help Roman, a person he barely knew and had no reason to like made Roman harder. The SEAL's no-nonsense attitude, his straight talk, his drive, and his commitment to helping Julia, rehabbing Sophia's lake house, and being a "brother" to Fletch enhanced Roman's attraction.

But the thing that resonated the most was that damn turtle story. Roman hadn't had a great aunt Sophia to help him during his emotional crises. He'd known from a pretty young age he was gay, and when he came out to his parents, their response had been less than ideal.

Not long before their divorce, Roman remembered the day well. He'd had a boyfriend in high school whom he was madly in love with. Thinking nothing of it, he invited him over for dinner.

Everything went well as long as his parents thought Jonah was a boy who was his friend, but the moment he reached over to hold Jonah's hand, his parents went off the deep end.

They kicked Jonah out after calling his parents to disapprove of the way they were raising their son. Roman had been banished to his room as his parents argued about which side of the family his gay came from. Not exactly how he imagined his coming out going.

Jonah never spoke to him again, which broke Roman's heart.

Over time his parents became less volatile and stopped giving him the daily lectures and sidelong glances. Mostly, they were soon too busy with their divorce to notice him. He turned to his grandfather, the one person who welcomed and celebrated Roman for who he was. He'd even walked in a Pride parade with Roman.

No, he hadn't had a Sophia in his life—he had his grandfather.

While his parents argued over the silverware and took chainsaws to furniture, Roman stayed with his grandfather, Reginald Furrow. Those had been the happiest days of his young life. His grandfather taught Roman everything he knew about business. Which, in the end, seemed to be his grandfather's plan, considering he'd left majority ownership of the company to Roman.

He remembered him saying "good sense had skipped a generation," and it wasn't until Roman took over the company he realized how bad things had gotten. Stephan Furrow had lost billions of dollars and almost half of their clients in his time as CEO. The man had no sense.

Looking down at his laptop, Roman responded to yet another request from Maxwell and his team. They wanted to take a team-building trip to Oahu of all places, and while he was all for team building, he didn't take trips to tropical locations. Besides, he doubted the legitimacy of their claim when he saw only the five original members were included, leaving out the three employees he'd sent to join the team.

Why they thought this shit would fly was clear. His father would've approved the request without a thought to its legitimacy or necessity to the company.

Once he was done shooting off the memo and sending it to Rick in the cloud, Roman saved the rest his work and shut down his laptop. His hardon had finally gone down thanks to getting absorbed in work. He pulled on his boxer briefs before sliding between the sheets. His eyes were already fighting to close as he looked out at the mansion on the hill.

The same three lights shone in the darkness like stars. The place was usually lit up when his father was home. The man didn't care about the cost of electricity or the environment. Again, Roman ran the possibility of his father being behind the murder attempts and hated knowing the bastard was capable of it.

Roman could use some of his grandfather's advice right about now.

Chapter Eleven

Brick's heart sped up when he heard the alarm from one of the perimeter sensors go off, followed by one of their traps crashing in the forest. The day was sunny and bright. Who in their right mind would try to sneak up on them now? Fletch ran out of the house and tossed Brick a gun before they passed the tree line.

"I told Julia and Roman to lock themselves in the cellar until we got back," Fletch whispered.

Brick nodded, already deep into hunting mode. His breathing was even though adrenalin was coursing through his veins. Their steps were deliberate and choreographed. His eyesight sharpened. Not a sound was made as they drew nearer to the trap that had been tripped.

A pair of white-tailed deer grazed upwind as he and Fletch navigated through the red cedars, bald cypress, and ash trees. The thick underbrush provided them with plenty of cover, but by the racket carrying on in front of them, it wouldn't have mattered what noise they made: the trespasser would never hear them coming. This wasn't some trained assassin, and when they moved in, it became clear why.

"Jake, what the hell are you doing on my property?" Brick growled with a healthy dose of rage as the out-of-shape man tried to untie his leg from the rope currently holding him suspended in the air.

"Get me down from here," Jake huffed as he gave up trying to free himself.

"Why should I? You're trespassing." Brick watched as Jake's face went an even deeper shade of red.

"I wanted a look, okay?" Jake grunted.

Brick looked over at Fletch, who shrugged his shoulders. "A look at what?"

"Whatcha guys were doing out here."

"Why would you care?" Brick asked. "Has someone sent you here to snoop around?"

"No. I want to know what's so important about this land."

"Simple, for me it's about family. For your former boss, it was all about ego."

"I'm thinking this is about Julia," Fletch growled.

"Yeah. Well, I have a lot of spare time on my hands now that Roman Furrow destroyed my business." His voice turned stone cold.

"You deserved what you got," Brick stated. "Had it been me, I would've dug a nice big hole out here in the middle of my ten acres."

Jake went silent.

"Stay away from this property. Do you understand me?" Brick warned. "There's nothing out here for you."

"Yeah. Loud and clear," Jake said in a more agreeable tone.

"Get the stalking bastard down while I call the sheriff," Brick said while pulling out his phone, which he'd turned off before entering the forest.

"Wait, can't we talk about this?" Jake scrambled. "We don't have to involve the law."

Brick shook his head and turned away. First, he'd call Roman and Julia to let them know it was safe to come upstairs, but for Roman to stay out of sight until Jake was dealt with. All they needed was for good old Jake here to go blabbing about their guest.

As he turned his phone on, he heard branches breaking behind him, followed by Jake cussing up a storm when he hit the ground. Brick turned around to find Fletch sheathing his knife on his belt, looking as innocent as a schoolboy.

"You didn't say how you wanted me to get him down."

Brick couldn't help but grin. "True."

***

When Julia's phone rang, Roman nearly jumped out of his skin. He and Julia had hunkered down in the cellar, which brought back a shitload of terrifying memories from the tornado.

Julia fumbled with the screen and Roman saw it was Brick calling. Without thinking, he grabbed the phone from her hand and answered it. "Hello."

"We found Jake, the real estate agent. It's safe to go upstairs, but I want you to remain in your bedroom until the sheriff leaves." Brick's voice was low and reverberated through Roman's body.

Without thinking he blurted, "Are you hurt?"

Silence. Roman was about to hang up, thinking Brick had already disconnected, when he spoke. "I'm fine, don't worry." Then Brick hung up.

Before Roman could analyze the change in Brick's voice, Julia was all over him.

"What did he say? Who's out there? Did they catch him?"

"It was Jake, your old boss. They have him," Roman told her what Brick said and handed her phone back to her.

Julia's eyebrows scrunched together. "Jake is trying to kill you?" she asked while crossing her arms. "That's weird."

"I don't think so. Brick didn't say, but he didn't seem worried. However, I did put Jake out of business."

"Thank you again for doing that," Julia said, and Roman heard the appreciation in her voice.

"You shouldn't've been put in that situation," Roman stated firmly. "I guess we'll find out what he's doing here after, but for now, we can go upstairs."

"Thank goodness for that," she said while unlocking the doors. "I never thought Jake was capable of something like that. Being an asshole bully, yes, but confronting someone stronger has never happened."

"People are strange, but I don't think it's him. My supposed bad luck has been going on for a long time, and I met Jake for the first time the day I met you."

They climbed the stairs back to the surface and headed for the house. It didn't make sense Jake would be here. If he was really behind trying to kill Roman, coming to the house in broad daylight was a suicide mission. Maybe his father sent Jake to do recon, though his father wouldn't know where Roman was. He was getting a headache thinking about it.

"You aren't like your father, are you?" Julia asked as if she'd had a line into his thoughts.

"I've worked extremely hard not to be anything remotely like him. Stephan is a narcissist who cares only about himself and what would serve him best. I never wanted to be like him when I was a kid, and as an adult, I distanced myself from him completely." Now his grandfather was a different matter entirely. Roman had always tried to emulate him and what he would do in most situations.

His moral compass was greatly influenced by his grandfather, who knew exactly where the line was between right and wrong.

***

Jake groaned as Sheriff Cooper loaded him into the back of his cruiser. Fletch sat on the porch eyeing the sheriff as if he were on the damn menu, and by the way Cooper was continually glancing over at the laser-focused redhead, the feeling might be mutual.

Brick didn't have time for this googly-eye shit. "If you two want a moment, I could leave?"

The sheriff sobered. "I'll get Jake booked in."

"What happens now?" Brick asked. "Slap on the wrist? Get out of jail free card?"

"No. Since Jake can't seem to stay out of trouble, he'll be spending a couple of nights as a guest of the county. After that, he'll be going in front of the judge to hear his charges and enter a plea before bail is set. If he bails out, there'll be conditions on his release, one of which will be to stay away from your property. Either way, I'll be in touch to keep you up to date."

"Thanks. 'Preciate it."

"You're fixing up the house. It's good to see Sophia's place coming back to life," the sheriff said as he took a long look around the property.

"You knew my great aunt?"

"Most people around here did. She was a kind woman," he said. "If you have any more problems with Stephan Furrow, let me know, and I'll come out and have a word with him."

"I'll keep that in mind."

"Another thing. Wanna tell me why you're setting up traps in the forest?"

Hmm, maybe there was more to this small-town sheriff than he'd originally thought. "I like my privacy."

"I can respect that. In what branch of the military did you two serve?"

"Navy SEALS. I'm going with a hunch, but which branch were you?" Brick asked, recognizing the signs.

"Marines."

Brick held out his hand. "It's good to meet a fellow veteran."

The sheriff nodded. "I mean it. Give me a call when there's trouble."

"When, not if?" Brick asked.

"That my hunch for the day," he said before tucking his notepad away, glancing back at Fletch, and then he got in his car. "Storms are being tracked in the area."

"Been a bad storm season this year."

"Hell yeah. Worst in five years." He backed his cruiser down the long laneway and, with a wave, headed back toward the road leading to town.

"What did he say," Fletch asked from directly behind Brick, making him roll his eyes.

"That Jake will be a guest of his for a couple of days. He'll let us know more after he's arraigned," Brick said as he headed back toward the house. He needed to check on Roman and Julia.

"That's it," Fletch whined. "Nothing else?"

"Look, your Marine now sheriff couldn't keep his eyes off you, which means one of two things. He's interested, or he's trying to remember if he's seen your ugly mug on a wanted poster."

"Hey," Fletch shouted.

Brick laughed even harder as he climbed the steps to the house. The moment he opened the door, his senses were filled with the aroma of coffee. When he rounded the kitchen table, he found Julia putting on another fancy attachment to her new toy.

"Are we expecting more company?" Brick asked as he took in the rows of different cups filled with various essential bean versions.

Julia turned around, looking more than a little sheepish. "I got nervous."

"Everything is fine. Jake won't be wandering around here again."

"Good. He deserves to be behind bars." She brightened up considerably at the news. "Um, would you like a coffee? I have cake?"

"Sounds like the perfect time for a break. I'll go get Roman," Brick said and then as he passed Fletch. "Help her set up, man."

"Definitely," he replied. "Where's the cake?"

Brick left them to it and walked down the hall to Roman's room. With a quick knock, he opened the door, which had Roman jumping up from his chair. "Sorry, it's only me."

Those dark blue eyes scanned him up and down as if looking for injuries causing something to click inside him. When was the last time someone worried about him?

"Is the sheriff gone?"

"Yes, he took Jake in. You're safe."

Brick watched as Roman's shoulders dropped, and he let out a deep breath. "Thank you. I didn't know what to think when I saw you running into the forest with your gun. I thought I might never see you again."

"Me?"

"Yeah," he replied before getting a hold of himself. "I mean, it was so dangerous, and who knew what was out there waiting for you."

"Of course, it's a scary situation. Julia is setting out coffee and cake. You want in?"

"That would be perfect," Roman said with a smile.

Brick couldn't stop the smile on his face if he wanted to.

Damn, he was in deep.

Chapter Twelve

The wind howled outside his window and whipped through the trees. The sky had turned grey hours ago as thunder clouds gathered filling the sky. Texas weather was changeable and could get dangerous at a moment's notice. Roman couldn't help but feel a bit on edge considering recent events. He prayed they didn't have to run for the cellar again.

It'd been a couple of days since Jake had been taken away, and everything had been quiet. Brick explained he had a couple of buddies digging up information in Dallas and tracking down leads. So far, they'd eliminated Rick as a possible suspect, which made Roman happy. He knew his friend couldn't be involved.

Unfortunately, his mother, father, and stepfather had not been cleared, making him feel sick. He'd provided Brick with an as accurate list as possible. Including men he'd dated from before the "accidents" started, and the cleaning service he used. He never had the time to clean, and he hated living in a chaotic environment. Having a service come in was well worth the money, unless they were somehow behind his assassination attempts. How bizarre to even have to think about that in relation to a cleaning company.

But he'd learned his house cleaner and two of his former lovers were cleared.

He couldn't help but wonder who these buddies of Brick's were. More than likely ex-military veterans. They seemed to gravitate to each other. Birds of a feather or something like that. Whatever it was, it felt like Brick had hired a detective agency, which was reassuring.

A branch came crashing down from a tree not twenty feet away and onto the grass. Roman couldn't stand it any longer and decided to see what Brick and Fletch were doing. When he came into the living room, he could see the trees blowing and bending in the copse off to the side of the house. It was all too familiar, and he couldn't stop himself from trembling.

The guys were sitting at the kitchen table watching the news and satellite radar, but he heard the words he'd dreaded when he went to join them.

"Do you think we should go to the cellar?" Fletch asked as Brick fiddled with the screen on his laptop.

Roman's mind went blank, and for some completely crazy reason, all he could think about was Sophia's rainbow turtle. He took off at a run in complete panic mode for the garden doors, hearing shouts as he rounded the corner of the porch, and picked up the heavy concrete turtle.

Quickly he spun around and ran back inside to find Brick and Fletch on their feet.

"What the hell?" Brick snapped. "You can't go out there in this storm." Then he looked down, and his expression softened. "What are you doing with that?"

"I heard Fletch saying something about having to go to the cellar, and I didn't think you wanted him left behind."

Brick was silent, making Roman nervous he'd done something wrong. The big man stalked across the floor and up to Roman. Before he knew what was happening, Brick wrapped his calloused hand around the back of Roman's neck and dove in for a kiss filled with passion and need. He gladly joined in, exploring Brick's lips and mouth. He tasted of coffee and pepperoni from their pizza earlier. Two flavors he wouldn't've paired, but on Brick, it was delicious.

"Um, if you two are interested, the storm has turned north, so we're in no danger." Fletch's voice broke in, and Brick pulled away. Carefully, he took the turtle from Roman and set it on the area rug. Then he stood and took Roman's hand.

He didn't care where Brick was taking him. Dazed from a kiss the likes of which he'd never had, he'd follow him anywhere.

When they ended up in Brick's room, he was ecstatic.

***

Brick pushed Roman against the wall. His need for this beautiful man drove him as Roman's groan's fed his ego. Fabric tearing drove his desire higher as the feel of warm skin under his palms sent shocks of want firing through his body.

He'd fought this attraction to Roman with everything he had, but Roman's pull proved stronger than Brick's usually unassailable will. Roman's hands ran up his ribs and carried Brick's shirt over his head.

Chest to chest had never felt as erotic as this.

When Roman ran outside in a panic, Brick didn't know what to think other than getting his ass back in the house. When Roman returned with the turtle, Brick could no longer hold back his feelings.

Roman took hold of Brick's nipple piercing and twisted it between his fingers until Brick's head nearly blew off his shoulders. How did this man have everything Brick ever wanted? With one kiss and barely into foreplay, no one had ever taken him this far into his desire before. But this wasn't only about sex. Something inside of him sought a real connection.

His head fell back as Roman's hand slipped between his jeans and stomach, taking hold of his cock.

"Damn, your touch is…," Brick groaned.

"Now I know why they call you Brick. Where the hell have you been hiding this monster?"

Brick chuckled low in his throat as he bucked his hips. "Want you."

"You have me," Roman growled as he pumped Brick's cock. "Fuck, this is crazy."

"Crazy is where I shine," Brick gritted out before reaching into Roman's track pants and grabbing hold of his sizable prize.

Shit, Brick was lost in a world of sensation and need. He'd never been stripped bare and accepted for who he was. Sure, a romp with a Navy SEAL was exciting, but no one had ever tried to dig deeper. Who could blame them when he'd likely be killed in some unnamed jungle? With his quiet demeanor and noble intentions, Roman had silently dug until the real Brick appeared, and then covered him in care and affection. There was no way he couldn't want the man he was supposed to hate.

"We need to get vertical fast, or I'm stripping you standing up," Brick warned.

Roman chuckled, shifted his weight, and tugged Brick until they fell back onto the bed. He sat up and grabbed hold of Roman's track pants from around the ankles and pulled them off the object of his desire before diving in.

Stripping out of his jeans took only seconds before he was skin to skin with Roman. Nothing and nobody had ever felt so good. He'd never felt so connected to someone he took to his bed. Their bodies melded together as if made for each other. There was nothing in this world to separate them.

The storm lashed against the windows as his hands roamed freely over Roman's body. Each muscle and ridge were touched with the kind of care he'd never shown anyone else. Tonight meant something. Roman meant something.

Feeling Roman's strong hands sliding against his body made him moan for more. While his brain tried to explain his actions, his body knew exactly what it wanted, but he had to make sure they were on the same page.

"I want you not only for tonight. I won't do halfway with you. If you have any reservations about exploring a commitment, you need to tell me now." If he was in, he was all in.

Roman looked up at him with those penetrating blue eyes as he ran his fingers through Brick's hair. "I want you too, but what about the distance between Dallas and Fire Lake? We can't ignore that."

"We can work that shit out," Brick said while rubbing his thumb over Roman's swollen lips.

"I want to, which scares the hell out of me, but for you, I swear I'll try."

Roman was willing to rearrange his insane life to include him. How had he gotten this fortunate, he'd never know.

"We can figure it out together," he whispered.

"Yes, together. Now, are you going to fuck me, or are we going to talk it out all night?"

Brick chuckled along with Roman. "Okay, okay. Talk is over."

"Show me what you got, Lieutenant Commander."

Had anything sounded so, right? He took hold of Roman's hands and raised them above his head. "They stay there."

Roman sucked in a deep breath and nodded as Brick straddled his gorgeous lover's body. All that skin laid out before him, Brick wanted a taste and lowered his head to lick Roman's right nipple, making him moan and his hips bucked.

When he sucked the peaked nipple into his mouth and lavished it with all his attention, Roman shuddered. By the time he raised his head to move further down Roman's delectable body, those piercing blue eyes were glazed with desire. He licked down Roman's chest and abdomen to the prize, a long, slightly curved erection. Roman was quite nicely endowed, and he knew he'd want to ride that in the future. But tonight, he'd be doing the driving. He wasn't exclusively a top, and with Roman, he'd want to feel him deep inside.

"Tonight, babe. You're mine, but sometime soon, I want to ride this beauty," he said as he pumped Roman's hard cock a couple of times.

"You'd let me?"

"Oh, yeah. With you, anything."

"Fuck. I'm going to explode if you keep talking like that," Roman warned

"I promise, you'll have more than one tonight."

Roman moaned but never moved his hands from the top of the bed. Brick ghosted his hand over his lover's balls, squeezing them before readjusting his position so Roman's legs were now spread wide.

He sucked Roman's cock down his throat relishing the distinct taste and feel of him, repeatedly pulling his hard shaft with his deep suction until he came with a roar. Gently he licked up the sides of his lover's still hard cock, making sure not to miss any.

"Brick, I need to feel you inside me."

"I need to prepare you. I don't want you to tear." With his girth it was a possibility, and he never wanted to cause Roman pain.

"Do you have supplies?" Roman asked.

"Yeah. In the bedside table."

Roman's face lit up. "Thank god."

Leaning over, Brick reached for his drawer, pulled out a condom and lube, and set them by Roman's hip. He released his lover's hands and nodded, indicating he wanted to feel them on his body more than he wanted to control. Brick had always needed control in all aspects of his life, but with Roman, he wanted give and take.

As Roman's hands left trails of fire everywhere they went. Brick reached over and squeezed a generous amount of lube on his fingers before leaning down for a kiss Roman readily gave.

"Ready?"

"Yesss. Take me," Roman replied, his voice a low rumble in his chest, which drove Brick onward.

"In good time." Brick said as he prepared to rock Roman's world.

From the first touch of his fingers to Roman's hole, his only mission was to send Roman flying on a wave of desire until he begged Brick to slide into him. All that mattered was Roman, and Brick centered all his concentration on him.

He slid one finger in and groaned at the tight warmth as he searched for the gland that would make Roman fly. The moment he found it, his lover's hands dug into the sheets, clenching tight as if he would fall off the bed without the anchor.

He slid a second finger in and pegged Roman's gland with every thrust. He watched the proper CEO as he came undone, and Brick drove on even farther.

"That's it. Take my fingers. Soon it'll be my cock."

Roman's legs opened wide and Brick had unfettered access. After his third finger slid in and he worked Roman until he was panting, Brick pulled out his fingers, rolled on the condom and lined himself up with Roman's stretched hole. The head of his cock pushed at the opening until the muscles gave way and allowed Brick to enter.

The feeling of warmth enveloped him, but he kept his slow pace even though he wanted to bottom out inside of Roman. He would never cause his lover pain and held on tight to whatever control he had left.

"Give me more," Roman begged, almost outdoing Brick's concentration. When he looked into those dark blue eyes, he smiled but stayed the course.

Slowly he inched his way in until his balls rested against Roman's butt cheeks, and he took a moment to enjoy the tight squeeze on his cock. With a nod from Roman, he pulled out slowly before sliding back in. Each time he went a little faster until they had a rhythm all their own.

Lightning flashed, brightening his room and covering them in light. The power went out, leaving them in darkness, but he didn't stop. He couldn't stop. It felt like the entire earth was rolling beneath them as it poured rain, rumbled thunder, and cracked lightning, urging them on to reach a peak Brick had never experienced. The flashes skittered across the ecstasy on Roman's face, and Brick took stronger hold of his lover's hips and increased his speed until his eyes rolled into the back of his head.

Releasing one side of Roman's hip, Brick pumped his lover's cock in time with his thrusts until Roman bowed off the bed, his come shooting across Brick's abdomen and chest at the same time Roman's hole clamped around him until he couldn't move and yanked his release from his body.

The roaring in his ears might have been him crying out, but so lost in the moment, all he knew was Roman was his. Slowly, he lowered his body to drape over his lover. Their breathing was labored, and neither spoke. Brick's brain had blanked and he couldn't make a coherent thought.

After several minutes, Brick he moved over to Roman's side, removed his condom, tied it off, and threw it into the trashcan. Then he gathered Roman into his arms and held him close while they recovered. The feel of Roman's arm laying across his chest and holding him close felt like what he imagined heaven would be.

"You meant it, right?" Roman asked.

"I mean everything I say, especially to you."

Roman snuggled closer and let out a small huff. "Good. I won't have to tie you down until you admit caring for me."

Brick's cock made a valiant effort to rise at the thought of tying down Roman, but his body wasn't up to it. They'd had a hell of a day, and this unexpected night had drained him dry. His eyes struggled to stay open, and when he heard Roman's soft snore, Brick allowed himself to fall asleep.

Tomorrow would be another day of trying to figure out who wanted to hurt the man he deeply cared about. Whoever it was better hope he never met them face to face. He wasn't sure he could control his actions, and for him, that was saying something.

Chapter Thirteen

Roman woke to an empty bed. The worst possible way to start the day after spending the night with somebody. Damn, and he thought everything had been worked out and wondered if Brick regretted sleeping with him.

Before he could tunnel down the rabbit hole of doubt, the bedroom door opened with a crack and Brick slipped through before closing it. In one hand, he had two mugs, and by the divine smell, it was coffee. Under his other arm was Roman's laptop.

"Good morning," Brick said as he set the coffees on the bedside table at the same time as he laid the laptop in the bed beside Roman. "How'd you sleep?"

Roman sat up, and instead of reaching for his coffee, he reached for Brick, who came to his side without reservation.

"What's wrong? You okay?" Brick asked as he wrapped his arm around Roman.

"Oh yeah. But I'd be better if you came back to bed."

"Wish I could, but your laptop has been blowing up. Pinging like crazy. I thought you might want to check it."

Roman opened the lid and saw a long list of emails. It wasn't even seven in the morning. He looked from his laptop to Brick and back again. With a nod of his head, he made an executive decision, the first of its kind.

"They can wait."

Brick's smile was priceless as he leaned in and kissed Roman, and then crawled back into bed, pulling him into his arms. Nothing had ever felt this right.

"Would you say we're dating?"

"We'd better be more than dating," Brick replied while motioning between them. "This is a committed monogamous relationship."

Roman couldn't help his joy at the sound of that. He wrapped his arms around Brick and hugged him as hard as he could. "Good."

For the next several hours, they talked about everyday things like family and growing up. Roman told him about his grandfather and his need to save the company if for no other reason than to uphold his grandfather's honor. Brick shared joining the Navy at eighteen and the SEAL Program at twenty, including some of the things he'd been put through in what sounded like torture not training.

It took more than eighteen months to go through initial training where he underwent a series of different specialties including water training, parachute jumping, and SEAL qualifications. Then, after he'd made it through all that, he was assigned to a team and underwent intensive specialized training for another twelve months before deployment.

The stats were serious. Of every thousand who joined, only around two hundred graduated. There was something called Hell Week where it sounded as if the trainers were trying to kill Brick. Seriously, the trainees were allowed only a few hours of sleep in twenty-hour cycles and were running over two hundred miles during their exercises. Then the trainers tried to drown Brick and the other trainees with their hands and feet tied.

Brick explained BUD/s and drown proofing. It definitely sounded like torture.

But the people who made it through were like Brick who felt it was an honor to wear the Trident: a privilege not many people could achieve. Crazy sacrifice. Roman couldn't understand it, but he respected it, and all the members of the armed forces.

"So, that would make you a super soldier?" Roman teased.

"Not a soldier." He made a face. "That's the Army. Those grunts can pound dirt all they want."

"You don't like the Army?"

"I like them just fine."

"But...."

"The forces tend to have monikers for every division, but only to be used if you've served. You can't go around taking jabs at someone in the Army without expecting to take it back. It's about rivalry and camaraderie.

"What do they say about SEALs?"

"That we're crazy and the cowboys of the military."

"Marines?"

"Leatherheads or jarheads."

Coastguard?"

"Puddle pirates."

"Navy?"

"Squid."

"Wow, you guys are harsh."

"As a bullet."

Roman laid his head on Brick's chest. "How close have you come to dying?"

Brick took a moment to answer. "Roughly three-quarters of an inch."

Roman's head shot up to look into those dark eyes. "Really? Are you joking?" He could feel his heartbeat speeding up at the thought of Brick not in the world.

"Nope. I was on a mission deep in-country looking for the leader of a terrorist cell targeting military bases."

"I never heard about that on the news?"

"And you never will. A lot of what we do civilians never hear about. A lot of our missions are covert. Hostage extraction is not something to be shared with the general public."

Roman shook his head. "Right. Damn. Scary shit."

Brick grinned. "One night we'd camped under a rocky escarpment, and when I woke up, I'd found I gained a new sleeping buddy. A Black Mamba."

"A snake?"

"A highly venomous snake with the ability to kill humans with one bite. It'd curled up on my chest. I imagine it was drawn to the heat. When I opened my eyes, we were basically face to face. I could hear my teammates moving around but didn't dare to take my eyes of the Mamba. I tried to get my arms out to grab its head before it had a chance to bite me, but that only angered it into raising its head high, exposing its black mouth and displaying his fangs as it hissed."

Roman felt his eyes go wide. "What did you do?"

"I couldn't do anything. We were in hostile territory and shooting off a gun would've given away our location. Thankfully, my teammates saw what was happening, and as the snake went to strike, a sizeable rock went flying over my chest, and sent the Mamba flying before it had a chance to bite me."

"Let me guess. It missed you by three-quarters of an inch."

"You got it. My teammates saved my ass that day."

"Well, I'm extremely happy they did. Now that we're... Well, I can't imagine my life without you in it. Isn't that odd considering we've only known each other a short while?"

"If it's odd, then so am I, 'cause I feel the same. Let's not think too hard on it and mess it up," Brick advised.

"Deal," Roman said while eyeing the clock on the wall. "I should start my day. It's almost noon, and Rick is probably having a fit."

"I'm happy your friend was cleared. I know how much it would have hurt you if he was responsible," Brick said before kissing the side of Roman's neck.

"Do you still think my family is involved?"

"We can't rule them out. It's not a secret you and your father aren't on the best of terms."

"That's a nice way to put it."

"True. Look at me being a diplomat." Brick shook his head. "Your old man has reasons, the wherewithal, and opportunity to come at you. He's been in your apartment and could've easily lifted your spare key. The same as your mother and stepfather."

"Is there anyone else left on the list other than them?" It couldn't be his family.

"Yeah. A man you dated named Daniel, and Detective Moses."

"Detective Moses?" Why would he be on the list?

"He's had your case for over a year, and we now know more than he does in no time at all. While his caseload might be heavy, it's not an excuse for not having come up with something. Either he's inept at his job, or there's a reason he's not finding any leads."

"I never thought of it that way. Your training shows. You guys see every angle."

Brick nodded. "It comes with years of knowing the evil in the world. I like that you don't see people the same way. You give them a chance. Me, I don't without solid reasons. In my career, that second chance could've gotten me killed. For now, the only people you can trust are me, Fletch, Julia, and Rick."

Roman couldn't say he was happy his "trusted" circle was so small. He hadn't lived his life looking over his shoulder. At least not when it applied to his physical well-being. Learning about Brick's training and knowing a little bit about the nature of his work made sense Brick didn't allow people to have second chances. But, even with all this going on, Roman knew his nature wouldn't change. He didn't want it to. He'd always try to give people chances, and Brick would make sure he didn't get carried away. Balance.

His laptop began pinging again, making him groan and lower his head. "Okay, okay. I'm up."

He rolled out of bed, threw on his track pants, and grabbed his laptop on the way out the door, followed by Brick's laughter. It was going to be a great day.

***

Having Roman sleeping in his bed at night this past week had helped with Brick's insomnia and night terrors. Every time he jarred awake, Roman's arms wrapped around him, and he managed to fall back to sleep. Better than any drug on earth.

But he knew there were times no one and nothing would be able to calm him, and he'd have to go onto the porch until his tremors stopped and the panic faded. The images that flashed through his mind never changed, even if the people did. His team was on a mission in a South American jungle and one by one his teammates were picked off until only he remained.

After a few moments, the scene changed and the jungle came alive around him as his teammates came lumbering out of the trees in various stages of decomposition. Then other people he hadn't been able to protect over the years of conflicts across the world followed his team in the same manner. They surrounded him, all chanting his name until the sound was crushing him, and usually, that's when he woke up in a cold sweat, his heart in his throat and his adrenaline pumping like he was in a combat situation.

His nightmares had grown more involved over the years as more people died. They too appeared from out of the jungle. Former combat brothers, refugees, families, mothers with their children, all blaming him for their deaths. No matter how hard he trained or how many people he'd saved, their accusing stares never changed.

PTSD was one of the many parting gifts for his service, along with a bullet scar on his leg and various other scars. This "gift" he'd give back in a heartbeat. He never regretted his service to his country, no matter how badly he was hurt. The injuries he carried with him meant someone else down the line wasn't hurting. A weird way to look at it, but it worked for him.

He pulled his truck into the grocery store across from the Marshall Pier and saw Jeff and Molly sitting with three other men with their fishing rods hanging over the railings. That must've been the fishing crew Jeff had invited him out to meet. Now was as good a time as any to introduce himself.

Brick jogged across the street and up onto the pier heading straight for them. Jeff saw him first, and by his smile on his face, Brick knew he was welcome. The other three turned in his direction, following their friend's sightline. Molly's tail started wagging as he got closer, and he noticed a bandage on her right ear.

"Brick," Jeff stood to greet him. "Glad you could make it out."

"Thanks for the invite. Can't stay long gotta pick up some groceries, but I thought I'd stop by to say hello."

"Guys, this is the Navy SEAL I told you about. Sophia's great-nephew who's fixing up the old lake house."

"Hey, I'm Tuck," a man who looked to be in his late fifties with a ZZ Top beard said as he held out his hand. "Army."

"Good to meet you," Brick said as he shook the man's hand.

"This here's Wreck, and Andy," Tuck said as he introduced the remaining two, who raised their hands in welcome. "Air Force."

Wreck fit him: eye patch, one arm. But Brick doubted that's how he got his name. Andy looked unscathed, but Brick knew looks were deceiving when it came to PTSD. Tall and slim, cleaned faced with hair high and tight, Andy hadn't let go of his military bearing.

"Good to meet you. How's fishing?"

"Horrible. Word's out, and the little bastards swam away," Wreck said as he tugged on his line a couple of times.

"It's too hot," Andy said. "They're off in the shade, where we should be."

"Would you like to have a seat, Brick?" Jeff asked as he unfolded a spare lawn chair.

"Sure, I can sit a little while," he replied and went over to join him.

"How's Sophia's place coming along?" Tuck asked.

"Slowly, but it's moving forward. If these storms would cut me a break, we could get shit done once instead of three times."

"Yeah, it's been one hell of a start to storm season this year," Wreck said.

Tuck sat back in his chair and looked straight at him. "You've seemed to have caused quite a stir around here."

"Stir?" Never give straight answers when someone was fishing for information.

"Yeah, with Jake and old man Furrow," Andy shared. "You put poor Jake out of business."

"Jake is the scum you wipe off your boots after trudging through a cesspool." Brick told them. "He bullies and threatens people who are weaker than him, forcing them to do things nobody should have to put up with in the workplace. The man should've never been allowed to carry on."

Wreck raised his can of Lone Star and said, "Here's to that. May the man rot in jail."

"Damn right," Jeff threw in.

"The new sheriff's been gunning for him for years, but his family has money in these parts. Enough for convictions to be rare," Tuck explained.

"What was with the poor Jake earlier?" Brick asked.

"Yanking your chain," Andy said. "Wanted to see how you responded."

Brick knew then and there he liked them. "What do you guys do for fun."

"We go out to the shooting range a couple of times a week if you want to tag along," Jeff offered. "Plenty of room. You can even bring that big redheaded guy we've seen coming into town."

"Fletcher's a former teammate."

"Hey," Andy said, holding up his hands. "Whatever you say. We don't judge," he assured him as he set his hand on Tuck's thigh.

"It happens to be the truth, but I'm sure my man will be happy to know."

"Bring him by sometime," Wreck said. "Be good to welcome him to town."

Brick looked at Wreck, and the older man smiled wide. "I know you're dying to ask?"

"Why do they call you Wreck?"

Andy started laughing, making all four of them laugh as well. The guy's openness was infectious, and Brick could easily see the affection in Tuck's eye when he looked at the man.

When Andy finally got himself under control, he said, "'Cause the crazy bastard could crash anything with an engine. From ATVs, and light tactical vehicles, to a Cougar 6X6."

"Story goes he was driving a Major General around the base when we were stationed in Iraq, and managed to take out not one, not two, but four flag poles directly in front of the mess hall. It was worth enlisting just to see Wreck shrugging his shoulders as the Major General stormed from the vehicle."

Wreck sat back with a smile. "Good times."

"Is that the cause of missing arm and eye?"

"You'd think," Wreck huffed. "Malignant Melanoma. Had a few tumors removed, but it metastasized, and they had to take the whole arm. Damn, live through hell and get taken out of the game by a lump on my arm. Doesn't seem right."

Brick had to agree. After all the things he'd seen and done, it would be a hell of a way to go out.

"And the eye?"

Wreck reached up and flipped the patch over, revealing what looked to be a healthy brown eye. "I think the patch makes me look dangerous."

The others broke out laughing again, and Brick joined along. He could hang with these guys. It was good to know other folks in the community, and he couldn't help asking one last question.

"Were you two out in the service?"

"No. We were in during the 'Don't Ask, Don't Tell' stupidity. It was okay to serve if you never divulged you were gay. If you did, you were discharged on the spot." Tuck shook his head.

"I understand. Even though things have changes, we still have to worry about reprisals and missed opportunities," Brick said.

"At least it's better than when you were considered to have a mental illness if you were gay back in the forties," Andy stated.

"Or when it was criminal," Wreck added.

"Yeah, times have changed, but in some ways, it hasn't." Brick said in reflection, happy he no longer had to have that worry rooted in the back of his mind now he was retired.

Yet, he couldn't help but think about the young people coming down the pike and their changes to the military.

One day being who you were wouldn't be clouded by stigma or hate. He hoped he was around to see it.

Chapter Fourteen

Roman watched Brick add wood to the firepit as Fletch handed him a beer from out of the cooler. The stars were shining, and the moon was only a sliver in the night sky. The sound of the water lapping against the shore rounded out the moment soothing him after a long day of virtual meetings.

He knew he'd have to make an appearance in the office sooner or later and wasn't sure how to broach the subject with Brick. His new lover was protective and likely to argue the fact or take him there in a tank.

"How's the world of business?" Fletch asked before taking a swig of his beer.

"Busy," Roman answered and used that as a catalyst to mention what he needed to say. "I'll have to go into the office sometime soon, though."

Brick's back straightened, and he turned away from the fire to look straight at him. "It's too dangerous. Did you forget how close that car came to ending you?"

"No, I haven't forgotten," Roman said through his teeth. "How can you think I'd forget that?" Hell, the sight of the car's grill would be forever stamped in his memory.

"Wow, that went fubar real fast," Fletch said before standing and walking back to the house. "Let me know when the fireworks are over."

Brick stood motionless for a moment before saying, "You're right. I apologize. That was uncalled for."

Roman's anger simmered. "You have to understand. Being the CEO means some things have to be done in person. There's a board meeting coming up, and I need to be there to provide a solid presence, or the company could lose the critical ground we've gained."

"I know how important the company is for you and your grandfather's memory, but I don't have to like it," Brick said. "I'm not leaving your side."

"That sounds fair," Roman chuckled before standing and joining his lover. Wrapping his arms around Brick made the rest of his anger fade away. He understood Brick's need to protect him, and Roman's partner needed to accept how much Furrow Investments meant to him.

***

Three days later, he was back in his office staring down at the pile of files lying in a neat stack directly in front of his chair.

"You like this style?" Fletch asked from his perch on an uncomfortable looking sofa. The back was black polished wood, and the seat was covered in thin hard foam wrapped in white leather. Not exactly built for comfort but, clearly expensive.

"No, it's my father's. I haven't gotten around to changing the," he waved his hand in a circle, "décor. I've had bigger fish to fry."

"Thank god, 'cause nothing like this is going into the lake house," Brick grumbled as he tried to get comfortable in a chair that would have fit better in some punk art exhibition than an office. The damn thing had spikes.

Even the thought of that made Roman shiver. "Definitely not."

Rick walked in without knocking, making both men jump to their feet.

"Easy G.I. Joes," Rick waved them off as he walked by. "Friend of the boss here."

Roman couldn't help but laugh at the confused expressions on the men's faces. Rick was one of a kind, and he wouldn't change him for the world.

"What do you have for me?"

"Only the latest numbers," he teased. "Hot off the press."

Roman took the papers and flipped through them with the speed of a trained eye. He couldn't believe what he was reading.

"We're up over all projections," Roman almost cheered. "Investors are returning to Furrow. We did it. After two long years, the tide has turned." His heart was racing. This was a sign. All his hard work was paying off.

"Your grandfather would be proud." Brick's sentiment added to his happiness.

The company was finally turning around, and people were trusting them with their money again. Roman would make sure none of their clients regretted their choice. He could finally breathe a little easier.

Things were coming together in his work life and personal life. Now—and he couldn't believe he was thinking this—if they could only figure out who was trying to kill him.

"The board meeting is in four hours. In the meantime, I need you to sign those," Rick said while pointing at the files. "They're marked, and here are some notes of interest that you asked me to compile before the meeting."

"Thanks. I don't know what I do without you."

"Remember that. I'm a size thirty-two waist, and I adore Gucci," Rick said as he sashayed out of the office doors, closing them behind him.

By the looks on Brick's and Fletch's faces, they didn't know what to make of his assistant. "You'll understand when you get to know him."

"Whatever you say, man," Fletch huffed.

Roman directed his attention on getting everything signed, and then he reviewed the information Rick had dug up before the board meeting.

***

Brick settled in as his man got to work. He pulled at his collar and necktie, trying to loosen them, but nothing helped. He hated wearing suits, even his officer's uniform, but he didn't want them to stand out in an office environment. He thought of it as another form of camouflage.

Fletch had fought putting on the suit tooth and nail but finally excepted his fate when Roman had told him he looked handsome. They had gotten more than a few stares when they came walking in on either side of Roman, but Brick didn't care. Whoever was after his man would have to get through him first.

After roughly an hour, Brick thought it would be a good time to walk the floor to keep an eye on things. "I'll go take a look around."

Fletch looked up from his magazine and nodded. Roman was so focused he didn't even move when Brick got up. Quietly, he opened the door and walked out into Rick's domain. His desk was set directly in the middle of the room and chairs were lined up against the two walls. Anyone approaching Roman's office would have to make it past Rick to get there. Good to know.

"Do you need anything?" Rick said as he stopped typing on his keyboard.

"No. I'm having a look around."

"Let me know if that changes," Rick said before going back to typing.

"You got it."

He looked out to the offices down the hall to the large open space. Offices with doors rimmed the middle of the room, which was comprised of cubicles. Brick was about to take a step forward when Rick spoke.

"You're not going to hurt him, right?"

Brick turned around and looked at him. "Roman? Never."

"I don't mean physically." He touched his chest near his heart. "He's one of the best people I know, and I don't want to see you playing with him. If you're not into this as deep as he is, don't lead him on. He deserves someone who's madly in love with him."

"Like you?"

"Ewww, no. That'd be like dating my brother. Sick. Yuck." He shivered.

Okay, that cleared that up. "I'm not in this to hurt Roman. I care about him, and I'm committed to seeing where this goes. I don't fool around. When I'm in, I'm in."

Rick's face softened, and Brick got a look at his less snarky side. "He's a good person, and I've seen men try to take advantage of him. I couldn't stand it if you were like them knowing how much Roman loves you."

"Loves me?" Bells went off. Way too soon for that.

"Oh shit, I shouldn't have said that." Rick turned away and made like he was suddenly interested in his framed portrait of Lady Gaga.

"He's told you he loves me?" Brick's heart was racing.

"Forget I said anything, and don't tell Roman." Rick waved him off as if he was trying to move on from over sharing.

"How can I forget something that important."

"Look, don't toy with him, okay?"

"Okay, I swear it." Brick was getting closer to understanding why this guy meant so much to Roman. Brick respected loyalty. It saved lives in the field.

"Isn't there some kinda code where you military men can't break your words?"

"It's more like respect, but for me, it is."

"Good," Rick gave him one more "I'll tear you to shreds" looks before returning to his computer.

Now that the interrogation was over, Brick moved into the office activity. Most of the women looked ready to attend a fancy dinner. Dresses, perfect makeup, and jewelry draping from their necks and wrists. The men wore suits, and not one was without a tie or perfectly cut hair.

Christ, he couldn't work like this. He respected those who did because it couldn't be easy to look perfect all the time, but shit, it'd be exhausting. As he made his way across the floor, he caught snippets of conversations but nothing of interest. Mainly names and numbers as a tickertape flashed across a long horizontal screen displaying stock prices. He didn't pretend to understand investing, that was Roman's world.

Spence and Shaw, his former teammates, were in the city lying low and watching their backs while they did what needed to be done. The sooner he was out of here, the better he'd feel. Then those two could return to chasing down leads.

When he reached the back wall, he found a display cabinet holding awards, like in high school. There were several awards with different organizations' names, and then there were ones for employees.

"That's mine," a female voice said from behind him. Brick didn't move. He'd sensed her nearing long before she got there.

"Congratulations," Brick replied before turning around to face her. "That must have taken a lot of work."

"Thank you. It did," she replied. "My name's Cheryl." She held out her hand for him to shake.

"Brick," he said. "Nice to meet you."

"Are you watching over Roman?" Interesting choice of words.

"Is that the latest scuttlebutt?"

Her eyebrows scrunched and lowered. "Military. My father was in the Navy and liked to use that term every time my sisters and I started fighting."

"Military brat?"

"And proud of it," she smiled. "You're going to protect Roman, right?"

"With everything I have."

Cheryl nodded and said, "Don't let anything happen to him. We can't go back to the way it was."

"We?" He asked before looking up to see more than a few eyes staring at him. "What was it like before?"

"It was a good ol' boys club. Which was perfect if you were white, male, and over fifty."

"Ah, I understand."

"Now that Roman has taken over, that club has been thinned, and we have more diversity. More people who'd been overlooked are moving into upper management positions."

"There's got to be some who aren't too happy about the changes."

"Maxwell and his team on the fortieth floor in allocations. Roman stopped their gravy train in its tracks. They weren't too happy at the new people the boss sent to join their division."

"I remember hearing something about him."

"Yeah, he's vocal about the new way of doing things and bashes Roman every time he gets. Most of us ignore him."

"Good to know." He may have to visit the fortieth floor this afternoon.

"Please, don't let Roman get hurt," Cheryl said before walking away and leaving him with a lot to think about.

Roman had mentioned this Maxwell character, and Brick quickly got the feeling the man had been given one too many second chances. He'd be damned if Roman's charitable nature would be abused.

One of the elevators dinged, and an older woman in a feathered hat came bursting out, heading straight for Roman's office. Brick pulled out his cell and gave Fletch the heads up before racing back down the corridor to head her off.

He knew by photos she had to be Roman's mother, Janice Furrow-Waters, but she hadn't been cleared, so she would not be getting any time alone with her son. Brick watched as she flew past a flustered Rick and threw the doors wide. By the time she took one step forward, Brick had reached her and cut her off.

"Get out of my way," she ordered. "I want to see my son."

"First, you go through me," Brick said as he glanced back to find Fletch standing in front of Roman's desk as the man tried to look around him. "I'll need to see inside your purse."

"My purse," she gasped as if Brick had asked her to strip naked. "You have no right to stop me."

"I have every right as long as Roman is in danger. Now hand over your purse. I need to check it for weapons."

"You think I'm involved in all of this nastiness," she asked while looking into the office, no doubt at Roman. "How could you think that of me?"

"Tone down the dramatics," Fletch said as he joined them. "It's simple. Show us the contents of your purse, and you can come in. The longer you argue, the more likely you won't be talking to your son."

"Well, I've never."

"Mother, do what they say," Roman sounded exasperated. "It's not the end of the world. You wanted me to have bodyguards."

"Fine," she said before thrusting her shiny white leather bag into Fletch's hands. "Look all you like."

Fletch didn't bother reacting to her theatrics. He opened her purse, looked around, and closed it again. "She's clean."

When he handed it back to the irritable woman, she pushed her way past them. "Unbelievable."

Fletch shook his head while Rick laughed. "The in-laws."

Brick couldn't help but smile back before shutting the doors. Hell of a first impression. The tally was now zero out of two when it came to the parents.

When he turned, he found her glaring at her son while she checked her purse. "Nothing is missing, mother," Roman said while rubbing his temples.

"You can never tell with this kind of riff-raff."

Fletch broke out laughing. "Am I the riff or the raff?"

"I prefer raff," Brick replied.

"Great, I'll be riff then."

Janice stopped and stared at the two of them. "Is this a joke? Tell me you haven't hired these two to protect you."

"I didn't hire them to protect me."

"Good."

"They're doing it for free."

Brick walked over to Roman's side, and his lover immediately took hold of his hand.

"Have you lost your mind? The board tolerates your choices as long as your choice is acceptable. I thought you wanted to save this company."

Brick was ready to bring this lady down a few notches when Roman squeezed his hand and took over.

"Mother, sit down." His voice had turned steel hard. This man was CEO boardroom Roman.

Damned if she didn't sit.

"You've known I'm gay since I was young. I don't hide it. I embrace it. As long as I run this company, no one will be ashamed of who they are. If you recall, you set me up with a man from the club, Mother."

She had the decency to look a bit ashamed, then she spoke. "That man was from a good family, and his last name carries weight in the right circles." She admonished Roman as if he were a child. "You should know better."

"You know, now I see it," Roman said, sounding utterly frustrated.

"See what?" she asked.

"What drew you and Stephan to one another."

"Don't say that." She brushed invisible lint off her sleeve. "It's just that all of this comes as a surprise. First, you have to be taken into hiding because someone's trying to hurt you. I don't know where you are, and if you're well. Then I hear that you came in for the board meeting without even telling me, and when I try to come to you, I'm treated like a criminal. It's all been quite a lot to handle."

Roman released Brick's hand and went to his mother. "This is my life, and you need to accept that."

"You know I love you," she sniffled.

"Yes, I know."

Janice wrapped her arms around Roman and hugged him. Brick could understand her surprise and defensiveness. It was a lot to take in. Still didn't mean she had a free pass, and he'd be keeping an eye on her.

Chapter Fifteen

Roman looked at the board of directors and waited as they reviewed the last bit of information and recent numbers. Policy changes and a new operating budget had been ironed out. Brick stood in the back corner of the room while Fletch was waiting outside the boardroom. Roman had to admit to feeling safer with them around.

He could concentrate on his work and not worry about what was waiting for him around the next corner. The meeting, as it was wont to do, had carried on late into the evening. All that was left was to adjourn until the next quarter.

"These are impressive numbers, Roman," Charles Avry said as he set his papers down. He was one of the longest sitting members of the board and had worked with Roman's grandfather. "Your grandfather is smiling down."

It felt like the weight of an elephant was lifted off his shoulders. It had taken years, but the company had finally turned around and was beginning to see serious profits. The Furrow name was beginning to shine again, and when he looked over at Brick, Roman saw pride in his lover's dark eyes.

This made the long nights and endless meetings worth it. The missed occasions and holidays, vacations and social life. It had all been worth it. Roman looked at the portrait of his grandfather hanging on the wall and could imagine him here at that moment.

This is for you, grandfather.

***

An hour later, when the last hand had been shaken and they'd returned to their hotel room, Roman loosened his tie and took off his suit jacket, hanging it over the back of a chair. They'd decided to stay at a nearby hotel instead of his apartment in case someone was waiting for him or had booby-trapped the door. It was more than exhausting to always have to think what was safe and what could get him killed.

They had adjoining rooms. One for Fletch and the other for him and Brick. Roman pulled his tie off and set it on his jacket. He'd hang them up in a minute. Brick walked in from Fletch's room and shut the door behind him. He looked beyond handsome in a suit. It was too bad the man wasn't comfortable, or he'd have him wear them more often.

"You look amazing in a suit."

Brick shook his head. "Not for me."

Roman walked over to him and undid Brick's tie, followed by his shirt and belt. "But you look so hot."

Brick's eyes widened. "Hot?"

"Definitely hot."

Brick began unbuttoning Roman's shirt, running the tips of his fingers along Roman's skin as he went. His lover's touch could bring him to the peak of ecstasy and make him beg with need. There was no other feeling in the world better than trusting someone completely.

Roman hadn't had that since he was young. When his parents turned on him when he came out, the stability he'd known had given way beneath his feet. Although they'd moved on, it still hurt. The last person he'd trusted this much was his grandfather. It was nice to feel that way again.

Brick began walking him back to the king bed, stripping him out of his clothing as they went until he was lying naked in the center of the mattress. He raised his arms, wanting his lover in the bed along with him.

Watching someone strip had never been erotic. With Brick, everything became sexual. Even toweling off after a shower. Brick's muscles stretched and bunched under his tanned skin like a well-choreographed dance. His tattoos were a roadmap of memories and hopes for the future, while his scars were a testament to war and the hardships he'd lived through.

No one held this much sway over him, and it didn't bother Roman in the slightest knowing he had the same effect on Brick.

"How did I get this lucky?" Roman asked.

"This old war dog? I think you have that the wrong way 'round. I'm the lucky bastard in this scenario," Brick said before falling into bed beside him. He reached over and pulled Roman close. "You mean everything to me."

"Are you worried we're moving too fast? That the rush of danger is making us go full speed ahead?"

"I've thought about it," Brick admitted. "Honestly, I fought my feelings for you with everything I had. If this was just a flash in the pan, it would've never gotten this far. You have a power over me I can't explain," he said before cupping Roman's cheek. "I love you."

Roman's heart skipped a beat before sense and oxygen returned to his brain. "I love you too."

"I know."

"How do you know?"

"Rick let it slip, but don't be mad at him. He was interrogating me at the time to make sure I knew if I hurt you, the wrath of Rick would be coming down on me."

"Did knowing how I feel make you say the same so I wasn't hanging out there alone?" Roman would be gutted if Brick was only saying the words because Roman had let his big-mouthed friend in on the secret.

Brick pulled Roman on top of him and looked him in the eyes. "The truth is you scare me."

"What?" Roman gasped. "How could I ever scare someone like you."

"Not physically. Mentally and emotionally. I've never allowed myself the luxury of loving someone. You are the first. Isolating myself started with my parents' divorce and morphed over the years into not wanting someone to worry about me, considering I could be killed on any mission. Then it became normal to live this way. Until you. I figured I'd lost the ability to love someone as deeply as I love you. Sure, I think it's fast, but I also feel it's perfect. I believe that with every fiber of my being."

Brick's unwavering gaze confirmed every word he said, which prompted Roman to say, "How about we're lucky to have one another. No one is more than the other. I've spent my life not trusting people because they could always turn on you. With you, trusting comes easy.

"Because you know I'd never hurt you, and I would never say what I don't mean. I love you, Roman Furrow. Completely."

A rush of warmth shot through Roman's body.

"I love you, too, Christopher Matthews." It felt so much more personal using his proper name. "Make love to me."

Brick's smile was instantaneous. "Whatever my man wants."

The remainder of the night was spent in each other's arms, loving, sharing, and exploring. Roman never wanted the night to end and wished they could stay like this forever.

Soon enough, the outside world would come crashing in, but until then, he would hold on to this moment and his astounding man for as long as possible.

Chapter Sixteen

Roman pulled up his jeans and went over to the counter over the little fridge. Damn, they'd gone through the coffee pods already. He never thought he'd admit this, but he missed Julia's elaborate machine. The ultimate coffee maker had spoiled him, and he wanted a lush cup of joe. But he'd settle for hotel pod coffee. He needed his jolt, and he knew Brick couldn't function without at least two cups of strong black coffee.

The shower was still running, and Roman smiled. They'd made good use of the large shower stall with multiple shower heads. A great way to start the morning. Brick had wanted to stay under super-hot pulsing water to iron at his "kinks," and Roman liked a warm shower, but not the scalding water Brick seemed to love.

Roman didn't want to bother Fletch with a simple coffee order so Roman went across the room to the little desk in the corner, picked up the hotel phone, and hit O. The operator connected him to housekeeping.

"Hello. This is room twelve-eighty-five. We need more coffee pods, please." The woman on the other end assured him someone would be there within five minutes.

While he waited, Roman finished getting dressed and turned on the news. When the knock came, he looked through the peephole and saw someone wearing a hotel cap and what looked like an oversized jacket. He opened the door and was yanked out of the room before he knew what was happening.

The barrel of a gun was shoved into his face and a voice that sounded vaguely familiar said, "Move. To the elevators. Now. You do anything but what I say, and I end you."

***

Brick walked out of the bathroom dressed and ready to hit the road for home. The quicker he got Roman back to Fire Lake, the better he'd feel.

"Roman, you ready to get going?"

Brick looked around the room, didn't see Roman, but saw the TV was on. He went to the connecting door and knocked to check if he was in there with Fletch. When Fletch opened the door, Brick walked into his room, and when he didn't see Roman his stomach dropped.

"Where's Roman?" Brick asked as everything inside of him went on alert. "He's not in our room."

"Don't know. Would he've gone somewhere alone?"

Brick went back into his room and scanned the area for any sign and saw the hotel phone on the side desk was pulled to the edge. He dialed the hotel operator who asked, "Do you need anything else sir? Do I need to reconnect you to housekeeping?" Brick told her "No" thanked her and hung up. He turned to Fletch. "He ordered something from housekeeping. Someone must've taken him when he opened the door."

"Shit." Fletch shook his head. "How many minutes do they have on us?"

"Ten at the most."

"Shit."

Brick dressed in under a minute, and stuffed his feet in his boots, figuring he'd tie them in the elevator.

Fletch took the stairs, and Brick stepped onto the elevator car and punched the lobby button. His heart was racing. Years in the service had shown him how evil works and what someone was willing to do to get what they wanted. Whoever this piece of shit was who'd taken Roman, had to've been lying in wait, saw an opportunity and took it. Somewhere in the hotel was an employee knocked cold or worse.

He was almost down to the lobby when he noticed something red on the hand railing on the back of the elevator. Moving closer, his stomach dropped when he ran his finger across the spot, coming away with what he was sure was blood.

The elevator doors opened, but Brick stood rooted to the spot.

"No one remembers seeing him leave," Fletch said as he held the elevator doors open.

"I think I know why," Brick replied as he pushed the stop button on the elevator setting off the alarm. "Call Detective Moses to get down here. We need him to get the hotel to let us see the surveillance cameras. Tell Moses to bring an evidence tech with him."

"What if he's the one who did this?"

"Then I doubt he'll answer. I'll call Spence and Shaw to regroup here."

"On it."

Brick struggled to remain calm. Roman was out there somewhere needing his help. "I'll find you. I swear on my life I will bring you home safe."

***

Roman opened his eyes and found himself alone in a small room. His head ached from where he'd hit it, and whatever shit was in that towel that was put over his mouth that'd knocked him out. It felt like a marching band was keeping time with a metal goth rock band in the back of his skull.

He had to blink several times to clear his vision before he could make out his surroundings. There were a few pieces of trash lying here and there, but there was no furniture. One window and one door stood in his way to freedom, but the metal bars over the window negated it as a plausible escape.

If he went out the door, he didn't know what was out there waiting for him. It wasn't as if he got a look at the person at his hotel room door. They wore the hotel cap low on their head, and the way too big from their frame jacket hid their identity.

Roman couldn't stand here and wait for whoever to come back, so he went to the door and turned the knob. Locked. Of course.

Footsteps began to come closer to the room, and Roman instinctively moved to the far side of the room. Not knowing who or what was coming through that door, he hoped the space would at least give him time to duck if someone shot at him. He heard the door unlock and watched as the knob turned.

The same person walked in still in the hotel uniform, freaking Roman the hell out.

"Who are you? What do you want from me?" he demanded, tired of this cat and mouse game.

The person reached up and pulled off the cap revealing someone he hadn't seen in a long time. "Daniel?"

"Hey, Roman. Miss me?" he asked in a scratchy voice.

Daniel's hands shook, and his cheeks were sunken in. His bloodshot eyes shifted back and forth, landing on one thing before quickly moving to another. He was jittery, and by the scabs scattered across his face and neck, Roman knew Daniel had moved on from cocaine to more powerful drugs.

"What do you want, Daniel?" he asked while trying to decide if he could take Daniel down. With him hyped up on drugs, it could lead to more violence, and Daniel had a gun. Roman didn't doubt Daniel would use it. Maybe he could talk some sense into him.

"Want? Money. Lots of money."

"Is that why you've been targeting me with those accidents?" Was it all about money?

Daniel looked confused for a moment, and something in his eyes changed. He smiled wide like the old Daniel and asked, "Hey Roman, what are we doing here?" Holy shit. He switched to a completely different persona. Too many drugs or mental illness—either way, Daniel needed help.

"We're leaving, buddy," Roman played along. "Let's go for lunch." He moved forward and was halfway through the door when Daniel grabbed him and shoved him up against a wall.

"Where the hell do you think you're going?" Daniel snarled while wrapping his hands around Roman's throat.

"Daniel, you don't want to do this. It's the drugs," he gasped. "I can get you help."

"Help," Daniel huffed. "I don't need help. I need money. I owe people you don't want to owe money to, and you're going to help me get it."

This whole thing wasn't making sense. Why would Daniel try to kill him when he needed Roman alive to withdraw the money? Drugs messed up people's minds, but even Daniel would know with Roman dead he wouldn't get a cent.

"Okay, I'll get you money," Roman coughed as Daniel's hands increased pressure on his throat. "We'll have to contact my bank."

When it looked like he would loosen his grip, it felt like the world exploded around him. A loud bang and smoke were filling the room. Suddenly Daniel's hands were gone, and Roman was being carried over someone's shoulder away from the smoke.

He heard the shouts calling out "Police" and let out a sigh of relief. It was the good guys. Once he was out of the building, which turned out to be an old warehouse, he was set down on his feet. Before the man turned around, he knew it was Brick.

Instead of wrapping his arms around him as Roman had hoped, Brick went into inventory mode, cataloging his entire body. Brick's hands stopped at Roman's throat. "Can you breathe properly and swallow? We're going to have to get that looked at in the hospital. Do you hurt anywhere else?"

"My head. I hit it on the elevator railing, when he held something over my mouth that knocked me out."

Brick growled. "We'll have you checked out to make sure it didn't cause any permanent damage. Other than that, how are you?"

"Okay, really."

"Good," Brick said, and then his demeanor changed. "What were you thinking opening the door to anyone? I was worried sick. Thank god we placed a tracker on you, or we might've never found you."

"Tracker?"

Brick held out his hand and said, "Wallet."

Roman dug it out of his pocket and handed it to him. Brick opened it up and pulled out his driver's license. On the back was a thin piece of plastic that reminded him of a circuit board.

"Why didn't you tell me it was there?"

"I slid it on there yesterday when we got back to Dallas, and you had enough on your plate to worry about. I would have told you today, but you were taken before I could."

Yeah, he'd messed up. "I'm sorry. I thought, it would be safe. I mean someone was coming up with coffee pods from housekeeping. It didn't dawn on me something bad could happen from something that simple. Obviously, I was wrong."

Brick's face softened, and he took Roman in a bone-crushing hug. "Don't ever do that to me again. In the darkest of jungles, I've never been as scared as I was when we realized you were gone."

"I promise," Roman said as he buried his head against Brick's chest. "At least now we know who it was."

"Daniel," Brick said with an unmistakable growl to his voice. "He was one of the people who had access to your apartment and the spare key."

"It's strange, though. All he wanted was money, so why try to kill me?"

"Drugs can make the strangest things seem normal at times," a voice said from behind him.

When he turned around, he found Fletch along with two other men dressed in black tactical gear.

"Roman, this is Spence, our information specialist," Brick said as he pointed at a man who was slightly shorter than the others but had the same muscled build and what looked like an assault rifle in his hands.

"Good to meet you. Thank you for saving me."

"And this is Shaw." This guy could be a movie star. He was gorgeous from his perfectly highlighted blond hair to a couple of days of expertly shaved stubble. With all of what he had going on, he did nothing for Roman even though he was sure men and women fell to their feet for a chance with him.

Shaw held out his hand with a megawatt smile and winked at him. Roman looked Shaw straight in the eye and said, "I'm not buying what you're selling, but I want to thank you for saving me."

The other men burst out laughing, including Shaw, as Brick pulled him back into a hug. "That's my man."

"I don't think we've ever met someone who could withstand 'the look.'" Spence laughed.

As Brick held him close Roman whispered, "Can we go home now?"

"To your apartment?"

"No. To Fire Lake."

Brick's eyes lit up, and his smile made Roman's stomach flip. "Yeah. Let's go home."

Chapter Seventeen

Another sunny day, and Brick listened to the melody of hammers and saws all around him. Spence and Shaw had decided to hang around the lake house for a bit, so they were assigned to replacing the boards on the waterside of the house, which had become weathered over the years and needed to be swapped out.

Thankfully, the lake house had plenty of bedrooms to house the ever-growing group. This was nowhere near what he'd expected his retirement to be like, but it felt right, and he didn't fight it. Everywhere he looked, something was being repaired, bringing Sophia's place back to life. He couldn't help but feel hopeful.

Roman came out of the house and was heading straight for him. It had been over a week since his kidnapping, and he seemed to be handling things well. Daniel was held without bail awaiting his court date, but investigators weren't getting far in questioning him. Years of drug abuse had done a lot of damage to his brain, and multiple personalities kept appearing.

"Hello, handsome," Roman said as he drew near.

"Hey. What's got you leaving your desk in the middle of the day," Brick asked, making Roman smile.

"I received a text from my father. He's back from Italy and wants to talk with me."

"When?" Something was up.

"This afternoon," Roman said.

"Why does he want to meet with you?" Brick didn't trust the old bastard. He was up to something.

Roman lifted his phone and pulled up the text. "It says he's been doing a lot of thinking considering recent events and wanted to touch base with me."

Brick noticed the hopeful look on Roman's face. The man was all heart. "I guess we can swing by later."

"Maybe it's best if I show up alone. I doubt I'll find out if there's a chance for some type of familial reconciliation if I bring you along. He'll likely clam up considering your last meeting."

Roman had a point, but it didn't mean he had to like it. "What if it doesn't go the way you hope?"

"Then I leave and never go back. I can't keep giving him chances."

Brick sucked in a deep breath before saying, "Okay. This is something you have to do, but I need you to do something for me."

"What?" Roman asked. He didn't know what Brick was going to say, but he trusted him to know it would never be anything to harm him. It felt good.

"I want you to text me when you get in the house to let me know you're okay." It was a hover move, but he couldn't help himself.

Roman smiled and hugged him close. "That I can do."

***

Roman drove his car to the front of his father's mansion and got out. He'd never imagined being back here, let alone so soon after Stephan had disowned him. He didn't bother knocking. His father knew he was coming, and Roman was about to send off a text to Brick when he noticed something was different.

He stopped in the foyer and listened. Silence. Where was the gaggle of women who customarily lounged all over the house? Where was Gerard, his father's butler?

Nothing was sending off warning bells, but he closed his phone anyway without sending the text. If no one was here, he'd turn around and go home. If his father was around, Roman would text Brick. He continued forward deeper into the house.

"Stephan?"

"In here, son." His father's voice came from the kitchen.

Son? Since when? He'd always called him Roman, avoiding the stigma of fatherhood Stephan couldn't stand. Then there was the disowning him thing.

Roman walked down the hallway and into the kitchen to find Stephan with his mother and stepfather. Stephan and Janice sat on the one side of the kitchen island closest to him, while Johnathan stood on the other side facing them.

"What's going on?" Roman asked. "You guys all in the same room makes me nervous."

"Don't be nervous," Johnathan said before lifting a gun from its hiding place behind the island. "Have a seat."

"Ah, shit," Roman growled as he sat beside his father. "It was you the entire time. Did you hire Daniel?" He never imagined his stepfather would be the one out to kill him. "Why are you doing this?"

"You'll be surprised to know Daniel was working all on his own. It happened to be a coincidence we were after the same person. Most of your accidents came from him, making all this possible for me."

"Johnathan, we can work this out," his mother pleaded as tears filled her eyes. "If it's money, you can have it."

"Money? I have money. What I want is power. You see, Furrow Investments is ripe to take off with the right man at the helm."

"Let me guess, you think that's you," Roman said disgusted with the piece of shit standing in front of him.

"Of course," he laughed. "As the only survivor of Stephan's psychotic rampage, I will take over and lead the company in my wife's honor."

"You think the board will vote you in as the new CEO simply because you married my mother?" Roman shook his head.

"Of course not. But as the beneficiary to Janice's shares and by trickle-down, Stephan's because you, Roman, are his beneficiary. However, with you dead, your shares would be left to your mother, and—"

"Since she's dead, it all reverts to you," Stephan said. "You little shit. How long have you been planning this?"

"Shortly after the old coot left Roman his shares. I was positive he would leave it to Janice, and then I'd simply have to make her disappear. But it never happened, so I had to wait to see if wonder-boy could bring the company back from the brink. Now that he has, it's time for a real leader to take over." Johnathan appeared too confident, making Roman even angrier.

While Johnathan continued with his spiel, Roman kept an eye on the large floor-to-ceiling windows. He *knew* Brick and the guys were out there somewhere. Roman had to make sure they had enough time to make a plan."

His mother sniffled. "Did you ever love me?"

"My dear, you were a means to an end. Besides, no one could take the place of your precious son. He's the only one you love, and don't even try to deny it."

"You honestly think no one will be suspicious you're the only survivor considering my father would've probably shot you first," Roman pointed out.

"True," Stephan said. "He'd be the first to go."

"Funny, but Stephan has been acting irrationally for a long time, and everyone knows it."

"Hey," Stephan grumbled. "You're the idiot with the gun."

"Janice has said on numerous occasions to anyone who'd listen that her ex-husband was insane. You couldn't have helped me out any better." Johnathan smiled. "Thanks to you, no one will ask too many questions."

"Bastard," Janice hissed.

Roman was sure he'd seen movement outside the windows. The guys were there, he knew it, and with his luck, that was when Johnathan pointed his gun straight at him.

"It'll be fitting I kill you first since your father despises you. Give him a little joy before it's his turn while digging the knife a bit deeper into my bride's cold heart."

"You sick asshole," Stephan spat, surprising Roman, considering Johnathan was right. His father hated him.

"It's been lovely knowing you all. I'll make sure to say a few kind words at your eulogies," Johnathan laughed, and all Roman could see was the barrel of the gun pointed right at his head.

The glass shattered, his mother screamed, guns fired, and Roman found himself on the ground with someone lying on top of him in a matter of seconds.

"Clear."

"Clear."

"Roman?" The sound of his name on his lover's lips had never sounded so good. But if Brick was calling his name, who was laying on top of him?

He shoved the weight off and spun onto his back to find Stephan lying on his side with a bullet wound in his arm. "Did you jump in front of that bullet for me?"

"You're still my son," he mumbled while holding onto his arm.

Brick leaned down and took Roman into his arms. "An ambulance is on the way."

"What about my mother and Johnathan?"

"Your mother is fine, in shock, but fine. Johnathan, on the other hand, won't be pointing guns at anyone anymore."

He looked up into those dark eyes and asked. "Is it finally over?"

"Yeah, I believe it is. But you're not allowed out of the house alone for an exceptionally long time. I've grown a ton of grey hair since meeting you. I don't need more."

"It makes you look distinguished," Roman said as he ran his fingers through his lover's hair.

"Right. We'll have to agree to disagree on that."

Sirens could be heard in the distance. The house was about to go crazy with the police and paramedics, but all Roman cared about was staying in his partner's arms.

"When can we go home?"

Brick smiled wide. "Soon."

Epilogue

The breeze coming in through the screened windows cooled the kitchen as five men sat playing cards while a summer shower blew through the area. Julia was elbows deep in a box of papers she'd found under Sophia's old bed when they'd finally cleaned out Sophia's room. His great aunt wouldn't want him to be mired in the past and knowing that truth had made removing her belongings a bit easier.

Even so, Brick couldn't let go of everything. Her favorite books, her hand-stitched American flag she'd made in his honor when he'd earned his Trident, numerous photo albums, and a few pictures. He'd asked Julia to look through Sophia's closet and take whatever she could use before the rest was given to charity. A young single mother would be the person Sophia would've wanted to have her clothing.

Julia seemed surprised but thankful, and mentioned she loved retro as she dove in. She did ask for one thing other than the clothes, the sewing machine stating she could make a lot of things for the house. Hey, if she wanted the alien looking device, she could have it.

The lake house was coming along a lot faster with the help of his former teammates. It hadn't all gone as planned, but he wouldn't change a thing. Brick set his arm on the back of Roman's chair as his lover dealt another hand. The man was remarkably stable and still working like a demon even after the chaos of a month ago.

The investigation into Johnathan Waters netted them a dirty cop. Detective Moses, it turned out, was earning a sizable salary from Waters to keep the investigation under wraps. From early on, Brick had suspected Moses seemed to have nothing helpful to share. It wasn't hard to figure out once Johnathan's accounts were analyzed where the money had gone. The idiot hadn't even bothered to hide the wire transfers.

Rick had been coming up to Fire Lake on occasion, deciding to check out the place his friend loved so much, and Shaw couldn't have been happier. The two were like oil and water, but Brick couldn't help but wonder if there was more.

Fletch was still silently lusting over Sheriff Cooper, neither having made a move since their first meeting. Spence had made himself a command center in one of the spare bedrooms citing the need for them to stay up to date. For what, Brick had no idea.

Roman's mother had taken her husband's betrayal and brush with death hard. Thankfully, she found a nice pool boy to while away her time as she recovered from her ordeal. While Stephan and Roman's relationship remained strained, both had agreed there might be something salvageable. Roman set the terms of their get-togethers, and Stephan had begrudgingly agreed.

To say Brick was shocked Stephan had taken a bullet for Roman was an understatement. He'd be forever in the old coot's debt for saving the man he loved, but it didn't mean he'd take any shit from him either. As long as Roman stayed happy with the new arrangement, Brick would support him, but the moment the elder Furrow tried to manipulate his son, Brick would put a stop to it.

It wasn't that he didn't believe Roman could take care of himself. More like he didn't deserve to have to deal with that kind of bullshit. There had been a few hiccups in the beginning, but Roman and Stephan were communicating.

As for his relationship with Roman, Brick couldn't have been happier. Even though Roman had to spend time in Dallas, their bond had grown even stronger. There wasn't a time when his lover wasn't somehow on his mind. He'd gone to Dallas on a few occasions, and they stayed at Roman's apartment, which was as modest as he'd claimed.

At times he worried things were going too well for him. Waiting for the other shoe to fall, but it hadn't happened yet, and he knew better than to expect it to stay that way. However, while it was peaceful, he'd enjoy his time with Roman by his side.

Shaw threw in his cards. "I fold. It's getting too rich for me."

Brick looked down at the stacks of pennies sitting in front of the man and shook his head. "Shit, I knew you were cheap, but this might be a whole new level. The bet's at three pennies."

"My mom used to say you gotta watch those pennies, and the dollars would take care of themselves," Shaw said as he crossed his arms over his chest.

"Bet she thinks you're cheap as well," Fletch laughed.

Spence pulled out his phone. "Let's call her and find out."

Shaw grabbed at the phone. "Don't call my mom?"

Everyone started laughing, and Spence put his phone away and took a deep breath. "What do you guys see happening now that Roman's safe?" he asked.

"Thank you for that. Honestly, I owe you guys everything," Roman said as he threw his cards into the pile.

"Happening? Like what? We all join hands and sing Kumbaya?" Fletch asked with his eyebrow raised.

"No, asshole. What do you all have planned?" Spence asked while looking around the table. "What are you going back to now that there's no need for us?"

The other men at the table quieted. Brick had to admit he wondered how much longer he'd have these guys around, and he didn't like the idea of them leaving. However, they had lives to return to. They weren't in the service anymore, and they weren't a team. Reality sucked.

"I guess I'll head back home get a job or something," Fletch said, sounding as happy about it as Brick was.

"Yeah, my dad wants me to take over the business," Shaw said, staring down at the table as if trying to burn holes into the wood with his eyes.

"I've been offered a position with the CIA," Spence said.

"You're going to wear a suit and tie all day, every day?" Brick asked with a shiver. There was something majorly wrong with that.

Roman sat back and listened but said nothing as each described a future Brick thought they didn't sound too happy about. Brick could see the gears turning in his lover's head.

"I guess you'll be staying here and finishing Sophia's house," Shaw said as he looked over at Brick.

"That was my plan."

"Okay, hear me out," Roman said as he leaned forward. "By the look of things, none of you seem overly excited about your options, and I know once Brick finishes the lake house, he'll be wondering the same thing you're thinking. What am I going to do that won't bore me to tears?"

"Agreed," Brick said as he pulled Roman's chair closer. "But nothing will separate us, don't worry."

"I'm not," Roman stated. "I'm never letting you go. What I'm trying to say is, why don't you guys all stay here?"

They all looked around at each other in question. It'd be great to have his teammates around after years spent fighting side by side. But then what?

"The house will be finished fairly quickly. Then what?" Fletch asked, looking unsure and repeating what Brick had thought.

"Well," Roman said as Julia joined them. "We been looking into a few possibilities, but we both agreed on one favorite."

Brick looked at Roman. "This is the first time I'm hearing this."

Roman reached over and squeezed Brick's shoulder. "We weren't sure if you guys would be open to it."

"What? We startin' some sort of strippers group," Shaw teased. "What else are we qualified for? I can understand wanting to see me naked, but these guys, I'm not so sure."

"No. It's not stripping," Roman said while shaking his head.

"What were you thinking we'd all do?" Brick asked, quieting everyone else.

"Julia and I have been looking into a possible business venture for the four of you. Investigations. Private Investigators and Protection services. Two things you're all highly trained to do. You can run it out of the lake house."

"I have the paperwork for you to look at," Julia said as the group remained silent.

Brick looked from his partner to the three men he'd trusted with his life on so many occasions in the past and considered them brothers. Case in point: recently the life of his love was placed in their hands.

They gave nothing away as if waiting for him to decide.

Did he want to start something new? He had Sophia's place to think about and his relationship with Roman. Even though he suggested it, doing this would surely pull time away from them being together.

"It'll be a lot of work," Brick stated the obvious to get a read for the room.

"Since when do you guys shy away from work?" Roman asked. "I understand it'll eat into our time, but I'm all in if it's what you want to do."

He loved Roman. The guy was, hands down, the best soul he knew.

"What do you guys think?" Brick asked the other three.

"Hard work's no problem," Fletch said with a grin and a flex of his arm.

"I've already got a command center set up in the spare room," Spence added while pointing down the hall.

"My dad can always have my younger brother take over the business," Shaw muttered.

"What kind of business does your dad own?' Julia asked.

"Insurance," he answered.

"You'd be good at that," Roman said with a laugh. "You could sell flood insurance to someone living in the Sahara."

"Thank you." Shaw beamed. "But I choose to use my powers for good."

"Oh brother," Julia huffed, causing another round of laughter.

Brick had missed the camaraderie of the military, but this right here was making up for it in a big way.

"You sure about this?" he asked while looking around the table. Roman, Julia, Fletch, Shaw, and Spence all had a say in this. "It could blow up in our faces."

"That's nothing new," Fletch reminded him. "I'm in."

"Hell, I'm in," Shaw said.

Followed by Spence stating, "Hell yeah."

He looked over at Roman and Julia. They looked at each other and smiled. "We've been in since thinking about this weeks ago."

"You're perfect for the job," Julia said. "With my organizational skills, I can make sure we don't run into any problems with licensing, billing, and such."

Brick took a deep breath. "Let's do it."

A cheer rose in the room, making Brick even happier about his decision.

"What should we call it?" Shaw asked. "Shaw and Associates," he suggested with a wiggle of his eyebrows.

"Military Men for Hire?" Fletch shrugged.

"Mega-Force Ultra," Spence suggested with his hands up in the rock horns sign.

Brick looked over at the only logical members and asked, "What have you two thought up."

Roman and Julia smiled wide before she laid a sheet of paper down in the center of the table. It was a drawing of a logo with a sleek, uncluttered design in black and white. Brick appreciated the design for its simplicity. They weren't fancy around here.

The center of the logo said, "L.H. Investigations."

He knew it was right the moment he saw it. "That's it."

The others passed the page around, and Fletch asked, "What's the L and H stand for?"

Brick smiled and answered, "Lake House Investigations."

Absolutely perfect.

ABOUT THE AUTHOR

M. Tasia is a M/M romance author who lives in Ontario, Canada. She's is a dedicated people watcher, lover of romance novels, 80's rock, and happily-ever-afters (once the MCs are put through their paces, of course), who grew up with a love of reading. She's a firm believer that everyone deserves to have love, excitement, and crazy hot romance in their lives. Love should be celebrated and shared.

Connect with M:
mtasiabooks.com
FB: mtasiabooks
twitter: @mtasiaauthor
IG: @m.tasia.author

www.BOROUGHSPUBLISHINGGROUP.com

If you enjoyed this book, please write a review. Our authors appreciate the feedback, and it helps future readers find books they love. We welcome your comments and invite you to send them to info@boroughspublishinggroup.com.

Follow us on Facebook, Twitter and Instagram, and be sure to sign up for our newsletter for surprises and new releases from your favorite authors.

Are you an aspiring writer? Check out www.boroughspublishinggroup.com/submit and see if we can help you make your dreams come true.

Love podcasts? Enjoy ours at www.boroughspublishinggroup.com/podcast

www.ingramcontent.com/pod-product-compliance
Lightning Source LLC
Chambersburg PA
CBHW051846170626
46807CB00003B/1372